DISCARDED

American
Eyes

American Eyes

. . . .

NEW

ASIAN-

AMERICAN

SHORT

EDITED BY

Lori M. Carlson

STORIES

FOR

YOUNG

. . . .

ADULTS

INTRODUCTION BY

Cynthia Kadohata

HENRY HOLT
AND COMPANY
NEW YORK

Henry Holt and Company, Inc., *Publishers since 1866*
115 West 18th Street, New York, New York 10011

Henry Holt is a registered
trademark of Henry Holt and Company, Inc.

Published in Canada by Fitzhenry & Whiteside Ltd.,
195 Allstate Parkway, Markham, Ontario L3R 4T8.

Library of Congress Cataloging-in-Publication Data
American eyes: new Asian-American short stories for young adults /
edited by Lori M. Carlson; introduction by Cynthia Kadohata.
    p.   cm.—(Edge books)
    Summary: These ten stories reflect the conflict Asian Americans
face in balancing an ancient heritage and an unknown future.
    1. Asian Americans—Juvenile fiction.   2. Short stories,
American—Asian American authors.   [1. Asian Americans—Fiction.
2. Short stories.]   I. Carlson, Lori M.   II. Series.
PZ5.A51146   1994   [Fic]—dc20   94-22391

ISBN-0-8050-3544-3

Designed by Victoria Hartman

First Edition—1994
Printed in the United States of America on acid-free paper. ∞
10 9 8 7 6 5 4 3 2 1

Permission for use of the following is gratefully acknowledged:

Blonde by Katherine Min. Reprinted with her permission.
Excerpt from *Wild Meat and the Bully Burgers* (Farrar, Straus & Giroux).
    Copyright © 1995 by Lois-Ann Yamanaka. Reprinted by permission of
    Susan Bergholz Literary Services, New York.
Housepainting by Lan Samantha Chang. Reprinted with her permission.
Home Now by Ryan Oba. Reprinted with his permission.
Summer of My Korean Soldier by Marie G. Lee. Reprinted with her permission.
Singing Apples by Cynthia Kadohata. Reprinted with her permission.
Knuckles by Mary F. Chen. Reprinted with her permission.
Fortune Teller by Nguyen Duc Minh. Reprinted with his permission.
Excerpt from *Bone* by Fae Myenne Ng. Copyright © 1992 by Fae Myenne Ng.
    Reprinted in cooperation with Hyperion.
A Matter of Faith by Peter Bacho. Reprinted with his permission.

Acknowledgments

American Eyes was compiled in the winter and spring of 1994, but my desire to do this book originated years ago. It is the product of my education, an education imparted by special people. I wish to name them here: Marie and Robert Carlson, my parents, followed by Dr. Wilton E. Bergstrand, Richard Kimball, Dr. Pablo Valencia, Dr. José Miguel Oviedo, Dr. William Sloane Coffin—all excellent teachers; and friends, Susan Demaske, Kathleen McGuire, Marjorie Agosín, and Vivien Chan. Thank you for being there.

I also thank my agent, Renée Cho, and my editor, Marc Aronson, for their support.

For Oscar,
who shares his vision
of the world with me

Contents

Editor's Note by LORI M. CARLSON   ix

Introduction by CYNTHIA KADOHATA   xiii

Blonde by KATHERINE MIN   3

Excerpt from *Wild Meat and the
    Bully Burgers* by LOIS-ANN YAMANAKA   8

Housepainting by LAN SAMANTHA CHANG   13

Home Now by RYAN OBA   28

Summer of My Korean Soldier by MARIE G. LEE   37

Singing Apples by CYNTHIA KADOHATA   49

Knuckles by MARY F. CHEN   62

Fortune Teller by NGUYEN DUC MINH   80

Excerpt from *Bone* by FAE MYENNE NG   108

A Matter of Faith by PETER BACHO   131

About the Contributors   143

LORI M.
CARLSON
· · · · · · · · ·

Editor's Note

Jasmine-scented airmail letters from my pen pal in Malaysia, tear-blurred images of Vietnam on my TV, orange-paper Japanese umbrellas, a shiny, lacquered black and gold-etched Chinese desk . . . these were, in my youth, the images I held of Asia. But who were the people behind these images and feelings?

My first encounter with anything Asian came when I was five or six years old, in the form of a desk. It was an American desk, actually made in Jamestown, New York, where I grew up. But it had been hand painted to replicate an authentic one, a desk from the land of China. It was beautiful, I thought. A shiny black veneer revealing scenes of Chinese noblemen by lakes, under a bamboo tree, in a palace—all in gold. The second drawer on the left-hand side was the special drawer. It was where my grandparents kept tiny, silver-wrapped chocolates for my sister and me; so we came to love that desk.

❀

Many years later, while studying at college, I invited my best friend to spend Christmas with my family. She was from Hong Kong. As it would be far too expensive for her to fly home to her own family, she accepted my invitation—but not before saying in a quiet voice, "Are you sure it's okay? Won't everybody stare at me there?" Her comment took me completely off guard. How could anyone not like her? She was smart and kind and pretty. All the same, she remained a bit apprehensive about going to what amounted to the *provinces*, where nearly everybody was of European ancestry. She told me that frequently people "gawked at her" in the Midwest, where we were attending school. That was in 1980.

In the past decade there has been a swift transformation of the cultural makeup of the United States. No longer comprised primarily of European Americans and African Americans, our society has become an increasingly colorful landscape of diverse religious and racial origins, flourishing side by side.

This anthology unveils a landscape where families of Chinese, Korean, Filipino, Vietnamese, and Japanese heritage are seeking their own place to thrive in our changing land. As the stories reflect, the process of assimilation has often been challenging. The very same sentiment that my Chinese friend conveyed to me about the way Americans perceived her a decade ago continues to be a concern among many Asian Americans—some of whom have written for this collection. When East meets West in the United States, the encounter is not always smooth. Any majority can be hostile, making fun of what doesn't look familiar.

Many of these stories return to a single theme: home. How can a home be safe and secure in a homeland that is dangerous because it rejects you for your difference, or because it invites you to be like everyone else? Is home the place that keeps the ways of another, more ancient homeland, or is it where new replaces old? In a nation where Asian Americans can change from black haired to blond, from cooking stewed pig's knuckles to craving fast-food hamburgers, from speaking pidgin to uttering standard English, where is home? Is home where we are different or where we learn to be the same?

The authors in this book describe many kinds of dialogues between home and homeland. Their stories, then, create a new kind of home on paper. For, really, there is no longer a clear divide between one culture and another. Asian Americans are changing the meaning of *American* as much as of *Asian*. They are using their own voices and visions— their American eyes—to Americanize all of us in new ways.

Introduction

I spent half my teenage years in Chicago, and for a long time after I'd moved, that city held a magical place in my memory. On several occasions in Chicago I spent the night outside, on or near the beach with boys and girls from school. We each told our parents we were staying at a friend's, and then we slept in an abandoned boathouse at Juneway Beach as the waves lapped up increasingly close; or we slept under the lifeguard canoes at Touhy Beach; or talked all night in a courtyard near the lake; or sat along a ledge overlooking the water. We brought cards, transistor radios, and cigarettes, and when the sun rose, we went home to bed. We all had homes and families, and I think what we were seeking was not escape, danger, or adventure, but magic.

As I grew older, life became more surprising all the time. I lost my virginity at a party. Grown men fondled my friends or me. One of my best friends had an abortion and became a born-again Christian. My family moved to Los Angeles, where I grew obsessed with what I looked like, spending hours at a time trying on clothes in front of my mirror. My high-school attendance record was abysmal, and at the beginning of my senior year I dropped out, simply walking off the campus of Hollywood High one morning between classes and never returning. I got a job as a waitress and felt despair.

The nights staying on the beach in Chicago were the last really magical times I was to have until I was twenty-five and took a bus trip up the West Coast by myself. This trip—the beauty of the coast and the variety of people I encountered— was a revelation to me. I had rediscovered magic. It was the next year that I decided to become a fiction writer. Then came the questions.

"What makes the work of Asian writers Asian?" "Do you think Japanese really act the way the characters in your writing act?" Those are some questions I have been asked in the last few years. I have been told that if the characters in a story are Japanese, then at some point whites *must* become an important part of the plot, for "conflict." I have been told by a magazine editor who wanted me to write about being Asian that she found herself "vaguely disappointed" I wasn't angrier. What all the well-meaning but somewhat absurd people who have asked these questions and made these remarks have in common is that they are trying to handle what shouldn't be handled. What they're doing is a little like pouring water on a fire in order to study the remains and understand why a flame burns. "Where would you place this fire in the postmodern tradition?" "What makes this fire an *Asian* fire?" I believe these people have lost the ability to perceive what burns, and so they resort to studying ashes. What I would like to do in this brief space is to look at what burns in these stories.

Home starts the fires in these stories. The authors write about rituals and language, about yearning for home, escaping from home, destroying home, losing and gaining home. A lot of people don't mind if you write about home, in fact they encourage it, but only if you speak Standard English, or only if you don't speak Standard English, or only if you are angry in a way that pleases them, or if they think you are *really* Asian. In other words, they want the ashes, not the fire.

There is no subject that is off-limits for an Asian writer, just as there is no subject that is off-limits to a writer of any race. A writer has no special obligation to his or her race unless such obligation resides in the heart. The main obligations writers have are to learn their craft and to keep themselves on fire. Only by fulfilling these obligations can they tell stories that burn. The way these obligations are fulfilled are an individual's business.

Just as the food you eat transforms itself into your life for reasons that are understandable yet ultimately cannot be understood, art moves both the artist and the observer in a way that is at once explicable and baffling. These moving and wonderful stories—full of the innocent fire of writers near the beginning of a hard road—prove as much.

—*Cynthia Kadohata*

American
Eyes

✾

Blonde

Blonde: dark yellow, gaudy as margarine; deep like a buttercup held to the chin; soft, the silky-headed down of chicks; the color of cold, precious metals like the shining luster of gold or platinum, silver-foiled and heavy; garish like an albino rock star's hair, not white out of age, but obliterating, like the sun that no one can look into because it is too hot.

We are a dark race, unified by a strict genetic conformity. Our great, great ancestors were Mongol horsemen who rode the desert plains of Asia in wild pursuits and conquest. The eyes, they say, are an evolutionary adaptation— hooded, small, angled slightly upward to thwart the spraying sand. Dark hair and skin to sustain the onslaught of unwavering sun.

The stories my father told me about ourselves. That God burned the first loaf, undercooked the second, baked the third golden brown; that we were superior people, smarter—civilization predating Egypt, five thousand years old, inventors of a printing press two hundred years before Gutenberg, of iron-clad battleships before the Spanish Armada.

I would have given it all to look like Lisa Ogleby. Graceful Lisa in her tartan skirts, with hair the color of gold, cut straight across and down, hanging in the collar of her soft cotton blouses. Her eyes were like quartz geodes, the blue in them too pale, seeming to give off light. She and I played with Barbies, also blonde, with nublike breasts that had no nipples. We dressed them in go-go dresses with white plastic boots and made them fall off furniture summits to meet strange, mangled deaths on the hardwood floor. Occasionally, we'd have invisible, vaguely imagined Ken men stage rescues, leading to embarrassing displays of gratitude on Barbie's part, stripped bare and rocking back and forth inside the dust ruffle of the living-room ottoman.

Once, Lisa's cat pounced on a Barbie, dragging it in her mouth as though it were one of her young. We chased her around the house, finally wrenching it free. Its left breast had been disfigured, the nub chewed almost clearly away, and there were sharp points embedded in her side like Saint Sebastian's martyrdom.

When we played together, I would hold Lisa in my sight like an assassin. I studied her movements, her laughter like low sneezing, the way her part was etched down the middle, revealing a reddish scalp. "Studying to be blonde," I called it to myself, should the occasion present itself. A story I told to others, that I believed myself sometimes— that I was adopted, my mother English or a Swede, beautiful, perhaps noble, blonde and blue-eyed and fair. I saw her in a tower window, memory from a picture book, vision from a fairy story. My father was a marauding Asian prince, descendent of the Mongol hordes, who swept her up in a conqueror's embrace, forcing her love with his proven courage.

Something strange, dimly understood, something to do with high tech, with science and the miracle of modern medicine, made it possible that my true identity was being hidden beneath the surface. That the dazzling blonde I was could be uncovered by a surgeon's blade, that underneath the black hair, the keenly adapted dark skin, was a girl of pure gold, Goldilocks or Shirley Temple, even, one day perhaps, Marilyn Monroe.

No one really believed me, of course, except stupid Doris Filcher, with whom I sat on the schoolbus. Her dry mouth opened, dull eyes widening to half dollars. She received my story as gospel, as the truest word ever spoken, and went home to tell her parents.

"My mom says you're making up stories," she said to me the next day. "She's gonna call your mom and tell her you're telling lies to people." She settled her hands primly in her lap and stared straight ahead.

"Don't lie to people," my mother said when I got home. "It's embarrassing."

"That's not the issue," my father said, impatiently. "The Filchers are unimaginative idiots. There's nothing wrong with making up stories. But you've got to be proud of yourself, Jean." He looked at me carefully. "You've got to like who you are."

Another ethnic feature—a flat nose. More adaptation to sand. Keep it close to the face and not a lot can fly in. It must have been very useful to my Mongolian forefathers. But we live in a fertile country with clearly delineated seasons and a rich, loamy soil. I lie in bed at night with a clothespin straddling my nose bridge. "Please God, make me a new nose, make me a new nose . . ." a whining, nasal prayer punctuated by gasping mouth-breaths.

Lisa Ogleby and I fought over the Barbie doll with the retractable hair, breaking the mechanism in her belly that made it work. She shoved me into the wall and stamped off to tell her mother. I held the broken Barbie in both hands. Its tangled hair would neither shrink nor grow no matter how I tugged and pushed, and I knew somehow it was hopeless, that whatever was wrong could never be fixed.

My father bought me a wig. It was lying on my bed one day when I got home from school, a cheap yellow thing that I mistook from a distance for a puppy, one of those low-to-the-ground rug rats favored by aging movie stars.

"You want to be blonde," my father said, "be blonde. Let's see."

I put it on with uncertain fingers—the hollow for the head was made of rigid burlap—and adjusted it awkwardly in the mirror, unable to discover the proper front of it. Shyly, I looked out into the image that was myself. My head gleamed; it sparkled; it reflected light like tiny strands of glass. The hairs were stiff and thick, golden wires of electric current that floated above my head. I stared at myself, tilted my chin, and smiled in Lisa Ogleby's sleepy way, as though her sunlit secrets had suddenly flashed into my brain.

My mother and father came in. They tried not to show it, but laughter welled up in them until they burst. They collapsed on the bed. They laughed and laughed until their eyes filled with tears.

I stared into the mirror, at my dark, centerless eyes, searching for Lisa's face, the blonde wig on my head like the usurper's uneasy crown.

LOIS-ANN

YAMANAKA

Excerpt from
Wild Meat and the Bully Burgers

*No one will want
to give you a job.
You sound uneducated.
You will be looked down on.
Listen students,
I'm telling you the truth
like no one else will.
Because they don't know how
to say it to you.
I do.
Speak standard English.
DO NOT speak pidgin.
You will only be hurting
yourselves.*

Jerry looks at me and puts his middle finger on the desk to Mr. Harvey. I tell him, "No, we gotta try talk the way Mr. Harvey says. No more dis and dat and wuz and cuz, 'cause we only hurting ourselfs."

I don't tell anyone, not even Jerry, how ashamed I am of pidgin English. Ashamed of my mother and father, the food we eat, chicken luau with can spinach and tripe stew. The place we live, down the house lots in the Hicks Homes that all look alike except for the angle of the house from the street. The car we drive, my father's brown Land Rover without the back window and my mother's white Rambler. The clothes we wear, sometimes we *have to* wear the same pants in the same week and the same shoes until they break. Don't have no choice.

Ashamed of my aunties and uncles at baby luaus, yakudoshi, and mochi-pounding parties. "Eh, bruddah Larry, bring me one nada Primo, brah. One cold one fo' real kine. I rey-day, I rey-day, no wo-ray, brah. Uncap that sucka and come home to Uncle Stevie." I love my uncle Steven, though, and the Cracker Jacks he brings for me every time he visits my mother. One for me and one for my sister, Calhoon. But I'm so shame.

Ashame too of all my cousins, the way they talk and act dumb, like how they like Kikaida Man and, "Ho, brah, you seen Kikaida Man kick Rainbow Man's ass in front Hon Sport at the Hilo Shopping Center? Ho, brah, and I betchu Godzilla kick King Kong's ass too. Betchu ten dollas, brah, two furballs kicking ass in downtown Metropolis, nah, downtown Hilo, brah."

And my grandma. Her whole house smells like mothballs, not just in the closets but all over. And her pots look a million years old with dents all over. Grandma must know every recipe with mustard cabbage in it. She can quote from the Bible for everything bad you do. Walks everywhere, she goes downtown Kaunakakai, sucks fish eyes, and eats the parsley from our plates at Midnight Inn.

And nobody looks or talks like a *haole*. Or eats like a *haole*. Nobody says nothing the way Mr. Harvey tells us to practice talking in class.

Sometimes I secretly wish to be *haole*. That my name could be Betty Smith or Annie Anderson or Debbie Cole, wife of Dennis Cole who lives at 2222 Maple Street with a white station wagon with wood panel on the side, a dog named Spot, a cat named Kitty, and I wear white gloves. Dennis wears a hat to work. There's a coat rack as soon as you open the front door and we all wear our shoes inside the house.

Now let's all practice our standard English, Mr. Harvey says. *You will all stand up and tell me your name, your grade, and what you would like to be when you grow up. Please use complete sentences.* Mr. Harvey taps Melvin Spencer on his shoulders. Melvin stands up slowly and pulls a Portagee torture out of his ass.

"Ma name is Mal-vin Spenca." Melvin has a very Portagee accent. Before he begins his next sentence, he does nervous things like fall off the side of his slippers and look at the ceiling and roll his eyes. "I am, I mean I wanna. I like. No, try, wait. I going be. No, try, wait. I will work on my gramma Spenca's pig farm after I grow up cuz she said I can drive the slop truck. Tank you."

No one laughs at Melvin. Otherwise he'll catch you on the way home from school and shove your head in the slop drum. Melvin sits down. He blinks his eyes hard a couple of times, then rubs his face with two hands.

Jerry stands up very, very slowly and holds on to the edge of his desk. "My name is Jerome." His voice, weak and shivering, his fingers white. "I in. Okay, wait. I stay in. No, try, wait. Okay, try, wait. I stay. I stay real nervous." His face changes and he acts as if he has to use the bathroom. He looks out the window to the eucalyptus trees beyond the school yard.

Jerry continues, "I am going be one concert piano-ist when I get big. Tank you." I'm next. Panic hits me inside like a rock dropped in a hollow oil drum.

Mr. Harvey walks up to my desk, his face red and puffy like a pink marshmallow or a bust-up boxer. He has red hair and always wears white doubleknit pants with pastel colored golf shirts. He walks like Walter Matthau. Mr. Harvey taps my desk with his red pen.

The muscles on my face start twitching and pulling uncontrollably. My eyes begin darting back and forth. And my lips, my lips—

I'm waiting, Mr. Harvey says.

Jerry looks at me. He smiles weakly, his face twitching and pulling too. He looks at Mr. Harvey, then looks at me as if to say, "Just get it over with."

Cut the crap, Mr. Harvey spits. *Stop playing these goddamn plantation games. Now c'mon. We've got our outlines to finish today.* Mr. Harvey's ears get red, his whole face like fire with his red hair and red face.

"My name is Lovey. When I grow up pretty soon, I

going be what I want to be and nobody better say nothing
about it or I kill um."

OH REALLY, he says. *Not the way* you *talk. You see, that
was terrible. All of you were terrible, and we will have to practice
and practice our standard English until we are perfect little Americans. And I'll tell you something, you can all keep your heads on
your desks for the rest of the year for all I care. You see, you need
me more than I need you. And do you know what the worst part
is, class? We're not only going to have to work on your usage but
your pronunciations and inflections, too. Geez-us Christ! It'll take
us a goddamn lifetime.*

"See," Jerry whispers, "you made Mr. Harvey all mad
with us. Now we all going get it from him, stupid."

I want to tell Jerry about being a concert pianist. Yeah,
right. Good luck. How will he ever do it? Might as well
drive the slop truck if you cannot talk straight or sound
good and all the *haoles* talk circles around you. Might as
well blend in like all the locals do.

Mr. Harvey walks past my desk. *C'mon, Lovey. Start your
outline. You too, Jerome.* Sometimes I think that Mr. Harvey
doesn't mean to be mean to us. He really wants us to be
Americans, like my *kotonk* cousins from Santa Clara. He'd
probably think they talked real straight.

But I can't talk the way he wants me to. I cannot make it
sound his way, unless I'm playing pretend talk *haole*. I can
make my words straight, that's pretty easy if I concentrate real
hard. But the sound, the sound from my mouth, if I let it rip
right out the lips, my words will always come out like home.

LAN
SAMANTHA
CHANG
· · · · · · · · · ·

Housepainting

The day before my sister brought her boyfriend home, we had a family conference over fried rice and Campbell's chicken noodle.

"This is the problem," my mother said. "The thistles are overpowering our mailbox." She looked at my father. "Could you do something about them before Frances and Wei get here?"

My father grunted from behind his soup. He drank his Campbell's Chinese-style, with the bowl raised to his mouth. "Frances won't care about the thistles," he said. "She thinks only about coming home."

"But what about Wei?" my mother said. "This isn't his home. To him it's just a house that hasn't been painted in ten years. With weeds." She scowled. To her the weeds were a matter of honor. Although Wei had been dating my sister for four years and had visited us three times, he was technically a stranger and subject to the rules of "saving face."

My father slurped. "Frances is a *xiaoxun* daughter," he said. "She wants to see family, not our lawn. Wei is a good *xiaoxun* boy. He wants Frances to see her family; he doesn't care about the lawn."

Xiaoxun means "filial," or "dutiful to one's parents."

I was almost to the bottom of my bowl of rice when I noticed my parents were looking at me. "Oh," I said. "Okay, I'll do it."

"Thank you, Annie," said my mother.

The next afternoon I went to work on the weeds. My father loved Wei and Frances, but he hated yard work. Whenever I read about Asian gardeners, I thought my father must have come over on a different boat.

It was a beautiful midwestern afternoon, sunny and dry, with small white clouds high up against a bright blue sky. I wore a pair of my father's old gloves to pull the thistles but kicked off my sandals, curled my toes around the hot reassuring dirt. Inside the house, my mother napped with the air conditioner humming in the window. My father sat in front of the television, rereading the Chinese newspaper from New York that my parents always snatched out of the mail as if they were receiving news of the emperor from a faraway province. I felt an invisible hand hovering over our shabby blue house, making sure everything stayed the same.

I was hacking at a milky dandelion root when I heard an engine idling. A small brown car, loaded down with boxes and luggage, turned laboriously into the driveway. Through the open window I heard a scrape as my father pushed aside his footrest. My mother's window shade snapped up and she peered outside, one hand on her tousled hair. I rose to meet the car, conscious of my dirt-stained feet, sweaty glasses, and muddy gardening gloves.

"Annie!" Frances shouted from the rolled-down window. She half-emerged from the car and shouted my name again.

"Wow," I said. "You guys are early. I thought you wouldn't get here until five o'clock."

"That was the plan," said Wei, "but your sister here was so excited about getting home that I begged off from call a few hours early." He grinned. He was always showing off about how well he knew my sister. But other than that he had very few defects, even to my critical thirteen-year-old mind. He was medium-sized and steady, with a broad, cheerful dark face and one gold-rimmed tooth.

My mother and father rushed out the front door and let it slam.

"Hi, Frances!" they said. "Hi, Wei!" I could tell my mother had stopped to comb her hair and put on lipstick.

We stood blinking foolishly in the sunlight as Wei and Frances got out of the car. My family does not hug. It is one of the few traditions that both my parents have preserved from China's pre-Revolutionary times.

Frances came and stood in front of my mother. "Let me look at you," my mother said. Her gaze ran over my sister in a way that made me feel knobby and extraneous.

Frances was as beautiful as ever. She did not look like she had been sitting in a car all day. Her white shorts and her flowered shirt were fresh, and her long black hair rippled gently when she moved her head. People were always watching Frances, and Wei was no exception. Now he stared transfixed, waiting for her to turn to talk to him, but she did not.

Still facing my mother, Frances said, "Wei, could you get the stuff from the car?"

"I'll help you!" my father said. He walked around the back of the car and stood awkwardly aside to let Wei open the trunk. "So, how is medical school?" I heard him ask. They leaned into the trunk, their conversation muffled by the hood. I looked at their matching shorts, polo shirts, brown arms and sturdy legs. When Wei came to visit, my father always acted like a caged animal that has been let outside to play with another of its kind.

Afterward, we sat in the kitchen and drank icy sweet green-bean porridge from rice bowls. Frances nudged me.

"Hey, Annie, I got you something."

She pulled a package wrapped in flowered paper from a shopping bag. She never came home without presents for everyone, and she never left without a bag full of goodies from home. It was as if she could maintain a strong enough sense of connection to us only by touching things that had actually belonged, or would soon belong, to us.

I looked at the package: a book. I stifled a groan. Frances never knew what I wanted.

"Well, open it," my mother said.

I tore off the paper. It was a thick volume about the history of medicine. This was supposed to be of great interest to me, because of a family notion that I would become a doctor, like Wei. I did not want to be a doctor.

"This is great! Thanks, Frances," I said.

"Very nice," said my mother.

"Ma, I left your present in my room," Frances said. "Let's go get it." They left the kitchen. My father and Wei began a heated discussion about Wimbledon. After a few minutes, I got bored and went to find my mother and Frances.

From the entrance to the hall I could see that the bedroom door was closed. I stopped walking and snuck up to the door on the balls of my feet. I crouched against the door to listen.

"I don't *know,* Mom," Frances was saying. She sounded close to tears.

"What is it that you don't know?" my mother asked her. When my mother got upset, her sentences became more formal and her Chinese accent more obvious. "Are you unsure that he really cares about you, or are you unsure about your feelings for him?"

"I know he cares about me," she said. She had answered my mother's question. There followed a pause in the conversation.

Then my mother said, "Well, I think he is a very nice boy. Daddy likes him very much."

"And of course that's the most important thing," said my

sister, her anger startling me. I wrapped my arms around my knees.

"You know that is not true." My mother sounded exasperated. "Your father enjoys spending time with other men, that is all. There aren't very many Chinese men in this area for him to talk to. He also likes Wei because he is capable of giving you the kind of life we have always wanted you to have. Is there something . . ." She paused. "What is wrong with him?"

Frances burst into a sob.

"There's nothing *wrong* with him. There's *nothing* wrong with him. It's just—oh, I just don't know—I don't know." She was almost shouting, as if my mother didn't understand English. "You and Dad don't think about me at *all!*"

I imagined my mother's face, thin and tight, frozen in the light from the window. "Don't speak to me that way," she said stiffly. "I am only trying to help you decide. You are very young. You have never lived through a war. You don't know about the hardships of life as much as your father and I do."

"I'm *sorry,*" my sister said, and sobbed even louder. I got up and snuck away down the hall.

My parents often mentioned the war, especially when I complained about doing something I didn't want to do. If I couldn't get a ride to the swimming pool, my mother told me about when *she* was in seventh grade and had to walk to school every day past a lot of dead bodies. My mother was a brave seventh grader who knew how to shoot a gun and speak four dialects. But what did I know? I'd lived in the Midwest my whole life. I ate Sugar Pops and drank milk from a cow. To me, an exciting time meant going downtown to the movies without my parents.

That night Wei and Frances and I went to a movie starring Kevin Costner and a blond woman whose name I don't remember. On the way to the theater the car was very quiet. When we arrived, I stood in line to get popcorn and then went into the dim, virtually empty theater to look for Wei and Frances. I saw them almost immediately. They were quarreling. Wei kept trying to take France's hand, and she kept snatching it away. As I approached, I heard him say, "Just tell me what you want from me. What do you want?"

"I don't know!" Frances said. I approached. She looked up. "Mmm—popcorn! Sit down, Annie. I have to go to the bathroom." Her look said: Don't you dare say a word.

I watched her hurry up the aisle. "What's wrong with her?"

Wei shook his head a minute, trying to dislodge an answer. "I don't know." My first time alone with him. We sat staring awkwardly at the empty screen. Then he turned to me as if struck by an important thought.

"Annie, what would *you* think if Francie and I got married?"

Despite what I had overheard between Frances and my mother, my stomach gave a little jump. I thought about what to say.

"That would be nice," I said.

"You think so?" Wei said eagerly. "Listen, can you tell

her that? I've got to convince her. It's like she can't make up her own mind. Why do you think that is?"

"I don't know," I said. "I guess she hasn't had much practice." Although I'd never thought about it before, I knew that I was right. *Xiaoxun* meant that your parents made up your mind. I pictured Wei wrapped up in flowered paper, another gift my sister brought back and forth.

Wei sat sunk in his seat, a speculative look on his face. "Hmm," he said. "Hmm."

I began to feel uncomfortable, as if I were sitting next to a mad scientist. "I can't wait to see this movie," I said quickly. "Frances and I think Kevin Costner is cute." I stuffed a handful of popcorn into my mouth. While I was chewing, Frances finally came back and sat down between us.

"How about it, Frances?" Wei said. "Do you think Kevin Costner is cute?"

I looked at Wei's face and suddenly realized that he could not look more different from Kevin Costner.

"Actually, Frances doesn't like him," I blurted out. "I just—"

At that moment the screen lit up, and despite myself, I gave an audible sigh of relief.

My father was waiting for us when we got home, under the lamp with the Chinese newspaper, in his sagging easy chair. This habit of waiting had always infuriated Frances, who felt compelled by guilt to return at a reasonable hour.

Wei greeted my father cheerfully. "Hi, Mr. Wang. Waiting up for us?"

"Oh no," my father said, regarding Wei with pleasure.

"I'm glad you're still up," Wei said, with a look of heavy male significance. "I wanted to talk to you about something."

This time I had no desire to listen in on the conversation. I headed for the bathroom as fast as I could. Frances hurried behind me.

"Aren't you going to talk with them?" I said.

Frances grabbed the doorknob. "Just shut up," she said. She closed the door behind us, and we stood for a minute in the pink-tiled room under the glow of the ceiling light. Frances leaned against the counter and sighed. I sat down on the toilet seat.

"You know," she muttered, "I really do think Kevin Costner is cute."

"Me too," I said. I stared at the tiny speckle pattern on the floor tiles.

From the kitchen we heard a burble of laughter.

"Dad really likes Wei," I said.

Frances sighed. "It's not just Dad. Mom likes him too. She's just too diplomatic to show it. Dad is more obvious." She raised her eyebrows. "At least I know exactly where I stand with Dad."

Her words frightened me.

"I don't get it," I burst out in spite of myself. "Why did you go out with him for four years if you don't really like him?"

Frances ran her hand around a water faucet. "He reminded me of home," she said. "Why did you sign up for biology instead of art class?" She slid quickly off the counter. "Come on, kiddo, time to hit the sack."

The next morning I slept late. Around eleven I was awakened by a muffled bang near my bedroom window. My mind whirled like a pinwheel: What on earth——? I jumped out of bed and pushed up the bottom of the shade.

Two male legs, clad in shorts, stood on a ladder to the right of my window. Then Wei bent down, his smile startling me.

He was holding a paintbrush.

"What are you doing?" I almost shrieked.

"Just giving your father a little help with the house," he said.

I pulled the shade down, grabbed some clothes, and hurried out of my room to find my mother. As I passed Frances's room, I saw her sitting on her bed, fully dressed, with a completely blank expression on her face.

My mother was in the kitchen, cutting canned bamboo shoots into long thin strips.

"Where is Dad?"

"Don't shout, Annie," she said. "He went to the hardware store to match some more paint."

"Why is Wei painting the house?"

My mother lined up a handful of bamboo shoots and began cutting them into cubes. "He's just being helpful."

"Why is Dad letting him be so helpful?" I couldn't find the right question. Wei must have asked my father if he needed help with the house. Why had my father consented? Why was he accepting help from an outsider?

My mother turned and looked at me. "Because Wei wanted to help, that's all. Why don't you go and wash up? You're thirteen years old; I shouldn't have to remind you to wash your face."

The next few days passed in a blur, marked only by the growing patch of fresh pale-yellow paint that grew to cover one side of our blue house and then the back. Wei worked steadily and cheerfully, with minimal help from my father. My mother went outside now and then to give him cold drinks and to comment on the evenness of his job, or something like that. Frances stayed in her room reading. I reported to her.

"Wei's finished with the back side and now he's starting on the garage," I said.

"Leave me alone," Frances said.

I went further into the room and stood in front of her until she looked up. "I said leave me *alone*, Annie! I'm warning you—"

"Well, why don't *you* say something about it?" I demanded. "Why didn't you tell him you didn't want him to do it?"

Her face contorted in something between anger and tears. "I can't tell him! He won't listen to me! He says he's just doing them a favor!" She bent over her book and flipped her hair angrily in front of her, shielding her face. "Go away!"

I left the room.

❀

With things at home going so well, my parents left the next morning on a day trip to Chicago. Every now and then they made the four-hour drive to buy supplies—dried mushrooms, canned vegetables—from a Chinese grocery there. After they left, we ate breakfast, with Wei and I making awkward conversation because Frances wouldn't talk to us. Then Wei got up and went out to the front yard. From an open window I watched him pry the lid off a can of paint and stir with a wooden stick from the hardware store. Frances went out on the front porch and stood at the top of the steps looking down at him.

"You can stop now, Wei," I heard her say.

He glanced up, puzzled.

"You don't have to paint today. Mom and Dad aren't around to see what a dutiful boy you are."

Wei didn't have a short fuse. He shook his head slowly and looked back down at what he was doing.

Frances tried again. "It makes me sick," she said, "to see you groveling like this around my parents."

Wei didn't answer.

"What is it with you?" she sneered.

Finally his eyes flickered. "My painting the house," he said, "is something between me and your parents. If you don't like it, why don't you go pick a fight with them? And why did you wait until they left to pick a fight with me?"

Frances's upper lip pulled back toward her nose. I thought she was sneering at him again, but when she turned back to the house, I realized she was crying. She looked horrible. She slammed the door, rushed past me, and ran into the garage, where she and Wei had parked the brown car. Then before Wei and I could stop her, she drove away down the street.

She came back in about an hour. I sat inside pretending to read a book, but Frances didn't reenter the house, so I figured she and Wei were talking out there. I was surprised when he came inside. "Where's Frances?" he said.

"I thought she was with you."

"Nope. Just finished the front. I'm about to put a second coat on the south side. Want to take a look?"

"Okay." I put down my book. We walked outside and around the house.

There stood Frances with her hair up in a painter's cap, busily putting blue back over Wei's work, painting fast, as high as she could reach. Two new cans stood in the grass. She had finished most of the side and had worked almost up to the corner.

Frances turned to look at us. There were splotches of blue paint on her hands and clothes.

"I liked it better the old way," she said. She glared at Wei, waiting for him to get angry, but he stood perfectly still. I felt cool sweat break out on my neck and forehead.

Finally Wei said, "If you wanted it blue again, you just had to tell me."

Frances threw her brush on the ground and burst into tears. "Damn you!" she shouted at Wei. "I hate you! You too, Annie! I hate both of you! I hate everything!" She looked at the house. "I don't care what color it is, I just hate everything!"

I took a step backward, but Wei walked right up to her and put his hand on her shoulder. Frances hid her face in her hands and sobbed. They stood like that for a long time, Frances crying and mumbling under her breath, and then she began to repeat one sentence over and over. I leaned forward, straining to make it out.

"Mom and Dad are going to *kill* me."

Wei looked relieved. "If we all start now, we can probably paint yellow over it before they get home," he said.

Two days later Wei finished the house. He and my father drove to the hardware store to buy white paint for the trim. I was sitting in the family room, listlessly leafing through a *Time* magazine, when Frances stopped in the door.

"Hey, Annie. Wanna go out and take a look?"

"Okay," I said, surprised by her sudden friendliness.

We walked out the front door, crossed the street, and stood facing the house. The street lamps had just turned on, and the house glowed gently in the twilight. Our raggedy lawn and messy garden were hidden in the shadows.

We stood for some time, and then Frances said, "I told Wei that I would marry him."

I looked at her. Her face was expressionless in the glow from the street lamp. Finally she turned and briefly met my eyes.

"It's not worth the trouble," she said. "Let's not talk about it anymore, okay?"

"Okay," I said. Without talking, we crossed the street and approached the house. It was a beautiful evening. My mother stood behind the kitchen window, washing the dishes. Frances walked smoothly at my side, her long hair flowing back in the dusk. I glanced up at the roof in a hopeful way, but the imaginary hand that had hovered over our home had disappeared. I blinked my eyes a couple of times and looked again, but it was gone.

"Come on, Annie," my sister said, holding the door. "Hurry up, or the mosquitoes will get in."

I took a deep breath and went inside.

Home Now

It was five in the afternoon and already the sun was going down. A jackknifed tractor trailer two miles ahead had traffic backed up to where Robert's Honda was—stuck under an underpass, surrounded by other cars. Robert hated winter, hated freeways, hated being where a sudden earthquake could drown him under a pile of concrete.

He was going to be late for dinner—that is, if his mom cooked any. More likely she was making some origami something or other that she and the other ladies sold to each other at boutiques. She wouldn't notice if he was late.

Robert had driven fifty yards in the last half an hour. There was no sign of this jam being cleared up in the near future. An old man in a Lexus cut in front of him and braked. Robert honked his horn. The driver didn't even look back. Robert pounded his steering wheel. It was getting late and no one was going anywhere.

❀

Then some movement ahead caught his attention. A few cars were skirting along the right shoulder to the next off ramp. Robert had never taken that exit, but what the hell? He was looking at a good hour and a half in this traffic jam and he didn't feel like going home anyway. Besides, he had a full tank of gas. With a shrug Robert cut to the freeway shoulder, to the off ramp, and into the city. . . .

Robert hardly visited the city. No reason to, really. A dirty place, full of gang members and bums. Yeah, he knew there were other things there, but he was mostly worried about the gang members and bums. He rolled up his windows and locked his door.

"My, what a beautiful part of Los Angeles," he muttered sarcastically. On both sides of the street was a tattered patchwork of warehouses and old brick buildings, some of them still burned out from the riots. He noticed a sign. Plain block letters on an orange Day-Glo background, it read IF YOU LIVED HERE, YOU'D BE HOME NOW. It was an ordinary sign, the sort of sign usually hung on a new apartment complex built next to any one of the various freeway interchanges. What made this one odd was that it was tied to a rusty chainlink fence surrounding an empty lot.

If you lived here, you'd be home now.

"Street artists at work." Robert snorted.

As he drove north, he began to feel strange. Somehow the buildings began to look familiar. He was sure he had never driven this way before. . . . Then he knew. Robert thought about the sign and began to smile. In a way, he was home. He remembered the area. Little Tokyo was just a few miles ahead.

Little Tokyo. Robert and his dad used to go there all the time. When Robert was young, they would walk up and down the street, looking at the Japanese stores and restaurants. His dad would tell Robert about the way the community used to be, before rich businessmen demolished the old shops to make room for their offices and hotels. Sushi was cheap back then; before the *hakujins* discovered it, you could get a plate for less than a dollar.

Of course most of the stores were gone now, as well as the bowling alley and the Atomic Café. At least that's what his sister told him. The last time he went to Little Tokyo was before his dad got sick.

Since his father's death, Robert always found one reason or another to avoid the area. He wasn't clear why; it just didn't seem right.

But today was different. Little Tokyo was ahead, and it was all he could do to keep his mind on the road. Maybe it was just one-too-many nights of coming home to see his mother in the living room surrounded by a pile of paper frogs or cranes or Japanese carp. She'd sit there, no lights on except at her worktable, not even looking up when he said hello.

Jeez—her crafts were everywhere—in the kitchen, in the bathroom, along the hallway. Even in his room—once he found a mobile of colored paper balls floating over his desk. When he took them down, the look on his mom's face made him feel so guilty he not only put them back, he asked her to make a pencil holder and paper-clip tray for him too.

But now Little Tokyo was ahead. J-Town. Just south of City Hall. His mouth watered at the thought of curry rice, beef teriyaki, and tsukemono. He was going to have a proper dinner, the kind his family used to have together at home.

It was one of those rare clear days in Los Angeles County that makes it impossible to get lost. To the east and north there are mountains, while to the west and south is the beach. In the middle of it all is the city. Usually the smog hides everything, but today the air was clear as air should be. The setting sun gave the glass skyscrapers a warm, other-worldly glow that made Robert think of revelation. He stopped at an intersection. This was different from the freeway. Seeing these golden buildings up close was almost like seeing the angels Los Angeles was named after.

Three streams of dirty water shot across his windshield.

"What the hell are you doing?" Robert screamed. He hit his horn and his accelerator at the same time and sped through the red light. In his rearview mirror he saw a bum holding a spray bottle and a wad of filthy newspaper.

As the figure shrank into the distance and it became obvious he wasn't going to shoot him, Robert felt safe enough to think.

"He was just trying to wash your windshield," he told

himself. And then, to no one in particular. "Lucky I didn't hit another car! I could've been killed!"

For the rest of the way Robert carefully checked each person on the sidewalk. He only let up his guard when he saw the tall pagoda marking the entrance to Little Tokyo. He laughed out loud at the sight.

If you lived here, you'd be home now.

It was amazing how a few Japanese signs could set off a space so completely. One block away, Robert wouldn't have felt safe enough to roll down his window. Here, though, Robert locked his car, fed the meter a few quarters, and started walking.

But it was more than the signs; it was the place. The sounds. The aromas coming off from the restaurants made his stomach growl. By this time the day was reduced to a soft glow in the western sky. The store lights were on.

After the war, this was the only part of the city they'd let us live in. It was the oldest, dirtiest part of Los Angeles, his father would say. *Look what we did with it. Look!*

Once he showed Robert the curb in front of an old noodle shop. There were iron rings coming out of the sidewalk. In the old days people would use these rings to hitch their horses. Robert forgot the name of the shop, and of course by now it had been demolished, but he looked for those rings anyway. He didn't find any.

Then his nose recognized a smell. A smell just like this one flickered from the past. It engulfed him, submerged him. Not teriyaki, nor candy, nor even perfume, it was the smell of old paper, incense, and mothballs. It was the smell of an old gift shop, where his dad bought him a book of Japanese fairy tales. "Momotaro." "The Rabbit in the Moon." And his favorite, "Urashima Taro." It had to be that shop; there was no other smell in the world like it. He felt a way he hadn't felt in a long, long time. He touched his cheek and realized he was crying.

For the better part of an hour Robert looked for that shop. Up and down First, Second, even Third Street, from Alameda all the way up to San Pedro. Nothing. New boutiques, gift shops, clothing stores . . . even a bakery whose signs were written in French. But no old gift shop. Robert frowned. It was like the ending of "Urashima Taro," when Urashima goes back to his home village after visiting the kingdom under the sea. Though it seemed like only a short visit, years and years have gone by. So when he returns, everything has changed and no one remembers who he is or any of his family.

A cold breeze sent a shiver down Robert's spine. It made its way to his stomach, reminding him that he hadn't yet eaten. Where to go? Most of the restaurants were new, and much more upscale than the small places he remembered. Investors from Japan had poured quite a bit of money into the area. And the buildings looked great— ceramic tiles, sleek marble, and new masonry. . . . Even in his business clothes, he felt a bit underdressed. What would his dad say if he saw this place now?

Oh well, thought Robert as he entered the closest restaurant, what would he think of *anything* if he were alive today? Of his wife filling their house with so many crafts that you couldn't take three steps without running into a box. Of his fishing poles, stuck in the garden, being used to grow tomatoes. Of his son, crying out in the open, for everyone to see.

As soon as he set foot in the restaurant, Robert knew they served good food. It was a fresh smell, delicately intertwined with hot tempura oil and just the right hint of tea. He went through the curtains into the restaurant. Nice.

Clean, like all Japanese establishments; paper lanterns were hanging from the ceiling. Energetic sushi chefs were busy rolling rice into California rolls.

"Irasshaimase!" greeted a waiter.

"Huh?"

The waiter looked puzzled. "Not Japanese?'

"Japanese American. I'm *yonsei*."

The waiter didn't acknowledge Robert's reply. Instead, his lip curled. "Not Japanese . . ." he repeated. He brushed him back into the lobby. "No room now! Wait."

Robert sat down and waited. A couple of Japanese tourists entered. They were very well dressed; their clothes looked like they were from France or Italy or someplace like that. The waiter greeted them and they were immediately ushered in.

"Maybe they had reservations," Robert tried to convince himself. He waited a little longer. The waiter peeked through the curtain and quickly looked away when he saw Robert still there.

The door swung open again. This time it was a Caucasian man dressed in a sweatshirt and blue jeans. The waiter ran over to him.

"Irasshaimase!"

The man looked puzzled and annoyed. "Do you have sushi here?"

"Oh! Sushi? You like sushi?" the waiter smiled a toothy grin. "Please come in, come in!"

Robert looked at the waiter in amazement as the other man was led into the bright restaurant.

If you lived here, you'd be home now.

Slowly Robert got up and walked out.

As soon as he left the restaurant, he heard someone approach him. He turned to see another homeless guy with his hand outstretched.

"Excuse me, sir, but I haven't eaten—"

"Well, neither have I!" Robert exploded. He stood there, surprised at the sound of his own voice. The homeless guy lifted his hands to cover his eyes.

"I'm sorry, man, I don't want no trouble."

Robert shook his head quickly, as if to clear the fog that had rolled into his mind. He pulled out a crumpled bill.

"Here, dude, take it," he offered.

"I don't want no trouble, man." The guy turned, then ran down the street.

❀

Robert walked the streets of J-Town as if in a daze. A dollar bill still held loosely in his hand, the hunger seemed to have left his body. He looked at the lights, the signs of the businesses, all in Japanese, a language he couldn't read. He looked past J-Town, to the skyscrapers of Civic Center. Those glowing buildings were dark now, save for bright halos of neon. So huge, yet so distant.

And there was that smell again, like a pair of old hands, quiet, yet familiar. This time, though, he let the smell sail past him, to find someone else, maybe, more worthy to follow its path. He passed a mural dedicated to the Japanese Americans who gave their lives for this country. He didn't stop to read the words.

He got into his car and retraced his route back to the freeway. It would be empty by now, everyone safely home from work, perhaps to wives, girlfriends, husbands, families. . . . His sister was probably painting in her studio, while his brother was in front of a computer somewhere. He thought of his mom, busy filling every emptiness with new children born of string, colored paper, and hot-melt glue.

The last thing he saw before the on ramp was that same orange sign, unreadable in the night. Still, he remembered what it said.

If you lived here, you'd be home now. As he drove, Robert expanded on the work of the artist—wondering how the sign would look in other places: in Japan, on a gravestone, in the kingdom under the sea . . .

MARIE

G. LEE

Summer of My
Korean Soldier

Being back in Korea, the land where I was born, was, in a word, sucky.

I had come here with this idea to learn Korean and, in my off hours, search for my birth parents, who were waiting for me somewhere in Seoul.

So far, though, all I'd met were a bunch of spoiled Korean Americans, *chae-mi kyopo,* who were spending their parents' money like it was water.

Korean classes weren't all that bad. But it was hard to be in a room full of kids who looked just like you, and have the teacher ask, "What's wrong with *you*? Why can't you learn this? You never heard it before?"

Actually, no, I said, and then the teacher, a well-meaning lady who sometimes got a little too excitable, looked really confused.

"Don't your parents speak Korean at home?"

No, I said. My parents are white. I am adopted.

And then she looked shocked and speechless. It was like all of a sudden she'd forgotten that she was in the classroom to teach, to pound Korean into our brains.

"Do you consider these Americans to be your *parents?*" she asked in amazement.

"Hey, I didn't know you're adopted," said Lee Jae-Kwan, otherwise known as Bernie Lee. "No wonder your accent is so fucked up. That must be so weird coming back here."

Yeah, it is, I said, and then I gave him a look that meant that I was through talking about this subject.

Even in the beginners' class, Korean rolled off the tongues of the students so easily. There was only one other person who sounded like me; she was a nun. And from France. And had blue eyes. She had a visible excuse. Our teacher would often sigh impatiently, make that woeful "haa" sound at both of us; but at me I saw her snatching secret looks, like you do through your fingers at gory scenes in *Texas Chainsaw Massacre IV* or something like that.

It bothered me that people like Bernie Lee, who never did his homework, couldn't read or write Korean for beans, who thought that the most important part of college was "the opportunity to party," would always speak Korean better than me, and would always, while we were here in Korea, feel superior because he was more Korean than me, whatever that meant.

The only Korean word I remembered from my childhood was *ddong,* the word for crap, *merde,* excrement. When I heard myself say it, it was the one word for which I had the perfect, clear, ringing pronunciation. Needless to say, I never had a chance to use it.

There was a time when I spoke better than everyone in the whole class. But those days are gone, and here I am marooned into this life, trying to make the best of it.

I can't blame Mom and Dad for adopting me—they wanted a kid. And wouldn't it be nice if Mr. and Mrs. Jaspers took a kid out of some poor Third World country? We'll name her Sarah, which means "God's precious treasure," they said.

Ever since I came over here, I've had what's been labeled a "bonding problem." It makes it sound like there's something wrong with my dental work. But what it really means is that I didn't bond with my parents the way I was "supposed" to. I found this out when I turned eighteen and could finally access my file in the social worker's office.

Frankly, I wasn't surprised. My earliest memories are of my Mom and Dad asking me if I loved them, and of me wondering what I should answer. And then they became panicky and, eventually, sent me to therapists and counselors all over town.

Why do they call this a bonding *problem*? Maybe I'd already bonded with my folks in Korea, and once was enough.

I like my adoptive parents though. I called them Mom and Dad, but I'm sorry, that's the best I could do for them. The best they could do for me was to live in an Edina neighborhood with only white people and their children who would later go to school with me and call me things like chink and gook and not include me in their games, their parties, their groups, their proms. Could anybody really blame me when I started staying in my room a lot, wearing black, getting my nose pierced at a head shop on Hennepin Avenue just because the spirit moved me?

I'm a virgin, though. Ha, gotcha.

God, I've got to find my real parents. They're waiting for me, and I know they feel as gut-wrenched about this as I do.

"You know what you need," my teacher said to me, "is to do a language exchange with someone—an hour of English, an hour of Korean a few times a week. It would improve your conversation."

I looked at her and felt very sore. Every night, from the dorm's study room, I could see Bernie and the other kids going out, dressed to the teeth and jolly. Sometimes when I woke at five to start studying, from my window I could see them getting out of elegant black taxis, stumbling to the door, then yelling in guttural Korean for the old *ajushee* to let them in, even though they'd broken curfew by a good six hours.

I wanted to be able to answer her in Korean, to say, "I'll think about it," in polite, precise Korean. But of course, I couldn't.

"I know a person named Kim Jun Ho, a friend of my younger brother's. He's at the university, although right now he's completing his time in the army. He wants to practice his English, and he would probably be a good teacher."

"Fine, fine, *gwenchana*," I said, more to get her off my back than anything. My eyelids felt sandy from staying up so late studying, and for the first time, I thought of quitting. Maybe after I found my parents I would.

"You don't need a language exchange," I said to Jun Ho Kim, who sat across from me and drank celery juice while I sipped at a ginseng tea that I'd tried in vain to sweeten with three packets of sugar.

We were at the Balzac Café. The neighborhood near school was full of these trendy coffee/juice bars that had the names of dead French authors: Flaubert, Rousseau, and around the corner, Proust.

Jun Ho seemed nice enough. He was tall, had short hair (because of the army, he said).

His English was perfect. He spoke with better grammar than half the kids I went to junior college with.

"No, no," he said modestly. "I want to improve my conversation, I want to speak like an American."

So in English, we talked about nuclear plants in North Korea, dead French writers, and stories he'd read about in some old American *Newsweek*s (for instance, he wanted to know how to pronounce *Hillary* and *Chelsea*).

When it came time to switch to Korean, we talked about the weather and studying. I ran out of words in about twelve minutes. He then asked me about my family, did I have brothers and sisters? What were my parents like? Even though he spoke wholly in Korean, I somehow recognized—but did not know—the words connected to family.

I answered, substituting the English word for every Korean word I did not know and basically ended up speaking in English. I told him how I was born in Korea but hadn't ever been back—until now.

"Are you sad?" he asked.

I shook my head. "No, because my family is somewhere in Seoul and I'm going to find them."

He nodded thoughtfully. "I will help you, if you want."

"Thank you," I said. "I'll keep it in mind."

Jun Ho's face then folded in on itself, like origami.

"It isn't, 'I'll keep it in *my* mind'?" he asked.

"No, it's not," I said. "I don't know why, but the expression is 'I'll keep it in mind.' "

He laughed good-naturedly. "I'll never learn English, it's too hard." He got up and paid the bill.

The first time I called the orphanage, the person who answered the phone hung up on me. The second time, too. It wasn't necessarily that they were being rude, but they spoke in Korean to me, I spoke in English to them, and this went on for a number of minutes, until the person at the orphanage hung up. It seemed to be a gentle, almost apologetic hanging up, though, as far as I could hear.

When I saw Jun Ho again, we went to the other side of the neighborhood to the Kafka Coffee House. He asked me, in English, about our secretary of state, Warren Christopher (it was lucky that I even recognized his name, much less knew anything about him). In the Korean hour, we talked about food (I had learned to order at restaurants) and studying. Then he asked me how my search had been going. I asked him if he'd help me, and he said he would.

We went to the closest pay phone, and he dialed the number. Soon he was talking in a continuous Korean from which I couldn't pick out any words. He looked at the piece of paper on which I'd scribbled my full name, as well as the Korean one that had been given to me at the orphanage: Lee Soon-Min.

He talked and talked. The longer he talked, the more hopeful I became—obviously the key to everything must be at the orphanage. Finally he hung up.

"What happened?" Excitement was flowing out of every pore.

"They cannot tell me anything over the phone."

"Huh?" I said. "What'd you talk about?"

"How to get to the orphanage, that kind of thing," he said.

"Can we go now?"

"I made an appointment for two weeks. That is the soonest someone can see you."

I sighed. My family was going to have to wait, again. It seemed unfair, but after waiting so long, I guess I'd have to do it. I'd also have to tough out at least another two weeks of this stupid Korean language school when what I really wanted to do was just take off, live with them, eat Korean food, and sleep in a Korean bed, and I'm sure my Korean would come back to me naturally. I admit I was starting to feel impatient.

The next time I met Jun Ho, he had his army uniform on, and he was also driving a car.

"How about if we do something different?" he asked, opening the door. I slid in. He grinned at me. Unlike the poker-faced seriousness of a lot of Korean men I'd seen, Jun had a dash of mischievousness, a kind of sparkle that flashed at you like summer lightning, where you can't quite tell if you've actually seen it, or if you've just blinked or something.

He pulled into the vortex of Seoul traffic as he explained that he'd borrowed a car from his friend so he could show me around a little bit. I was suddenly aware that I'd seen very little of Seoul besides the immediate neighborhood of the school, so I sat back, pleased.

"Next week is the orphanage," I said. "You'll come with me, right?"

He cracked another grin at me. "Right now we will have fun," he said. "We will talk only about fun things."

"Okay, later," I said agreeably. I wondered if things would be different when I could speak Korean. Would there be things I could say that I couldn't before?

We went to the Sixty-three Building. It's called that because it has sixty-three floors, or it's supposed to—I didn't count. The top floor has an observation tower. We got lucky, because during the humid summer the city is pretty much always obscured by industrial smog; it had been raining the last few days, and today the air was mountain clear.

The observatory was a whole floor, and you could walk all around it. Having been mostly on the ground between tall buildings, I'd forgotten about the mountains rising along the sides of the city. Now they loomed in all their majesty, forming a ring around the city. When I'd flown in and seen those mountains—so familiar, somehow, so much like home—I'd started crying.

I leaned and looked out for a long time. Somewhere out there was my family. On what side of the Han River would they live? Would they be rich? Poor? I thought of how each ticking of the clock brought me closer to them, and I felt happy.

At the souvenir shop there, Jun Ho bought me a pair of figures that looked like warped, demented totem poles. At the top, each one had a monster head. It was not pretty to look at. Jun Ho said that these were miniature versions of ones people used to erect outside their villages to scare the demons away.

"Will it scare my demons away?" I asked.

"It might," he said.

We stepped into the elevator, where a young woman bowed mechanically to us before pressing a white-gloved hand to the button for the lobby. You couldn't feel any motion in the elevator as it descended. When the doors opened and the familiar lobby scene appeared, I felt like I'd been beamed in from another planet.

The day for my appointment came, but before we went, Jun Ho sat us down at the Kafka.

The orphanage had very little information, he warned me. They wouldn't be able to help me find my family.

I jumped up, wanting to hit him. What nonsense was he talking about? He'd talked so long on the phone, made an appointment for me.

Sarah, he said. There was no news. He'd made the appointment for two weeks hence in hopes that perhaps I'd give up on my own.

It's better this way, he said. Perhaps better for your family.

How could that be? I yelled. My family is waiting for me. You're just like all the rest—keeping me from them.

I think that's when I collapsed back into my chair, sobbing. I think I might have knocked over the sugar bowl, too. Koreans don't show their emotions, especially not in public. *What a crazy foreigner,* they were probably thinking.

"We'll go," Jun Ho said. He took my hand, and we caught a taxi.

The orphanage was filled with babies. There were loud, shrill cries, the smell of unwashed baby bottoms. The heat pressed down on my shoulders almost unbearably.

But this was my last hope; I had to push on.

A woman in a severely tailored Western-style suit met

us. Jun Ho told her who I was and handed her my letter of
introduction from the social services agency in the States.
She stared at me hard, as if trying to make the connection
between me and those squalling babies.

"I told her you want to see your file," Jun Ho explained.
I leaned into him gratefully. There was always that hope, I
was thinking. Something undiscovered in that file.

She brought out a file folder that had a few sheets of
paper filled with single-spaced Korean writing. My heart
jumped. There had to be something in there. . . .

"Please read it to me, Jun Ho," I said. "Read every word."

Jun Ho scanned the page, then looked up.

"Sarah," he said. "It doesn't say much. It just says about
your eating habits and so forth."

"Read it to me," I said, desperation beginning to crawl
up my back. "Promise me you won't leave anything out."
My whole Korean life lay among those spidery interlocking
symbols.

Jun Ho looked at me again. His eyes were so black, they
were liquid. He lowered his head and began to read.

" 'A newborn baby girl was found on the steps of the
Hoei Dong fire station on July 12, 1974. There was no note
attached or any other kind of correspondence indicating
any relatives.' "

Jun Ho paused, but I urged him on.

" 'The baby was found covered with feces . . .' "

Ddong, I was thinking. I know that word. The baby. I
was that baby.

" 'The baby appears to have been born in a toilet, or some kind of commode . . .

" '. . . cleaned her up. A name of Lee Soon-Min was given . . .

" '. . . was placed in foster care . . .

" '. . . was adopted by an American couple, Sue and Ken Jaspers.' "

I couldn't see anymore. It was like the day I stood behind a waterfall and tried to look out at the lake. Minnesota has more than ten thousand lakes.

Today was July 12. "It's, like, my birthday," I mumbled.

Jun Ho took my hand. He was leading me back to a cab. He barked directions to the driver, a large oily man who looked back at me, my tears and some stray hairs clogging my mouth. Jun Ho barked something else, and he started the car.

"Where are we going?" I surprised myself by speaking in Korean.

Jun-Ho only smiled and gave my hand a squeeze.

"Home," he said.

Out the window, the rows of tiny stores were pressed together so tightly that they looked like one continuous, rickety storefront, save for the different signs in Korean writing each had in front of it. As the taxi picked up speed, the signs began to blur.

CYNTHIA
KADOHATA
. . . .

Singing Apples

My grandmother—my mother's mother—surprised my family by dying one night in a motel in California. Neither my three brothers nor I liked our grandmother. She harassed us by boxing our ears whenever it occurred to her to do so, and she devastated us with her insults and her predictions of ghastly futures for all of us. We traveled a lot, and sometimes in the car she would talk on and on, until even my mother would get annoyed and tell her to keep it *down,* just as if she were one of us kids.

Sometimes my father did farming work and my mother helped out, other times he found work at a garage or as a carpenter. We usually traveled in the Pacific states with one or two other young Japanese families, heading for jobs the fathers had heard of. It was always hard to leave our homes, but once we started traveling, there was a part of me that loved our life. All that packing and moving was especially hard on my parents, but I think even they enjoyed

some of the long drives—at least they did when my grandmother was quiet. I liked driving through the passage of
light from morning to noon to night.

When we were on the road, my brothers and I woke
every morning at six o'clock when our grandmother—
Obāchan—took us for a walk. We had to go with her unless we weren't feeling well. Some days, whomever we met
on those walks would be the only people I talked to besides
my family and whatever family we were traveling with.
Those walks were one of my favorite parts of growing up.

Early the day Obāchan died, she woke us when it was
still dark gray out. She wanted to take a long walk. My father's job—at a farm—wouldn't be finished until evening,
and we had nothing to do all day.

We put Peter, who was two years old, into a stroller and
headed off through a sloping field and some orchards. Peter
was used to bumping along. He could sleep through anything.
A fine mist broke up our view, as if each drop of mist were a
dot of paint. The mist sprayed coolly on our cheeks as we
walked through the field, and the long misted grass brushed
our ankles. Though the oldest child, I was also small, and so a
slow walker. I could feel the blood flowing to my face as I
tried to keep up with Obāchan, who always walked briskly.

She had a cigar and stopped to blow smoke rings into the
air. The sky, white-gray, showed through the rings.

"Will you smoke when you get older?" Ben asked me. Ben
was the lively, talkative one. Walker hardly ever talked, except to repeat something just said. Sometimes we called him

"Echo." He had the sweetest face I'd ever seen. Ben was eight, Walker seven. I had just turned twelve.

"I'll never smoke," I said. "I want to be the opposite of Obāchan. Anything she does, I never will."

"She eats," said Ben. "And you have to eat."

I chased him through the grass, but he stopped abruptly and knelt, and I fell over him. I rolled, just for fun, through the damp field, and when I got up and looked back, Obāchan and my brothers stood rigidly watching me. With them was an old man. How had he appeared so suddenly? And from where? No matter; he was here now. We all turned to him, but he didn't speak. Though facing him, my family and I were looking at each other, not physically, but sort of emotionally. I felt aware of them, felt they were aware of me. I think traveling as much as we did had somehow given us that constant awareness of each other.

The man's face did not appear old, but he had wispy white hair that stood on end, seeming to move and fly of its own accord like something alive.

Obāchan didn't speak. There was something imperial about the way she held herself, the way she ignored the man. She appeared to be looking through him, at the sky and the fields. I could see that Obāchan wasn't going to speak, so I told the man I hoped we weren't trespassing.

He chewed on something and glanced over the beautiful misted fields. The fields were full of pale greens. They were his fields, I felt sure. "Maybe you're trespassing," he said.

"Sorry."

He chewed some more. The wind blew at his hair. I thought the wispy strands might fly away. "But maybe you're not," he said.

Obāchan continued to gaze through him. "We'll go now," I said. We turned and began to leave. I noticed Obāchan's cigar was gone. I noticed something burning a hole in her pocket. Obāchan, whom I lived in fear of, was scared of this man.

"Hey," the man called, and we turned around. "I'll sell you some apples cheap."

Everyone looked at me expectantly. I was the oldest child, so it was my responsibility to answer. "What kind of apples?" I said.

"What kind do you want?"

"Well, are they good?"

"The best."

The hole in my grandmother's pocket had stopped smoking.

Ben pulled at my arm. "I like red apples," he said to me. "I like yellow ones, too. I don't like green ones."

"Do you have red and yellow ones?" I said.

"Just happens to be what I got," the man said, suddenly grinning.

It was okay; he just wanted to sell some apples.

Men had come out to work some of the fields, and the men watched us pass. They touched their hats when they said "Good morning" to me and my grandmother, and I felt very grown up.

"Where are you all from?" said the man.

"Here and there." My grandmother had told me once never to tell people where I came from, or what my name was.

He nodded at her. "She speak English?"

I considered this question. Maybe she didn't want me to tell. "I'm not sure," I said, stupidly.

"We've lived in Fresno," said Ben. "We just came from Oregon. That's where I was born."

"Hmmm," said the man. "I've never been to Oregon, but I've been to Washington. Same difference."

"You're ridiculous," said Ben, only he said "ridictalous." I socked him, as he'd known I would. He giggled.

Behind the farmhouse sat several bushels, a couple of them filled with large Golden Delicious apples, sunbursts of pale rose and green on the rich yellow skins. We pooled our money—Obāchan had most—and bought two dozen apples.

"You know how to pick the good ones?" said the man.

"How?" said Ben.

"No, guess."

"Color?"

"Nope."

"Smell?"

"Nope." He paused before saying with mock impatience, "Do you want me to tell you or not?" He paused again, throwing an apple into the air. Finally he said triumphantly: "Sound." He squeezed and rubbed the apples between his large hands until the apple squeaked. "Good one," he said. "It sings. Never buy an apple unless it sings." He added hurriedly, "Of course the ones you just bought are all good." He rubbed and rubbed, making three distinct notes, enough for "Mary Had a Little Lamb" and another song I didn't recognize, and he moved his head in time with the music, his hair following the movement of his head. We also tried to play the apples, but ours sounded like tiny sick cows.

We headed back without the man. The workers in the fields stopped again to touch their hats.

"Hey!"

We turned around, saw the man standing in the distant mist.

"Someday you teach your kids that apple trick!" he called. He tapped at the space above his head as if he wore a hat, and then he walked off with his dancing hair, and with his singing apple still in hand.

He'd given us no bags, and we had trouble carrying the apples. Obāchan walked way ahead with Peter. We kept dropping the apples, but after a while we were having so much fun chasing after the falling fruit that we began to drop them deliberately. As I chased a stray apple, I saw that Obāchan had stopped walking, and I thought she wanted to scold us. But she was staring out over the fields, the way you might stare at somebody you love as he's leaving you. My grandmother had worked on a celery farm between her first and second husband, and I wondered whether she was remembering that. When I think back on how she looked, I believe I knew then that she would die soon. But when we caught up with her she slapped the side of my head. "Why did you give that man my money?" she said.

That evening when my father finished work, we started driving immediately. We were going to visit with relatives in Los Angeles, then head to Arkansas, where my father had a job that he hoped would be permanent. The Shibatas, a family we'd met that week, were traveling with us to L.A. We stopped for the night at a small motel. That was a long time ago—the motel cost two dollars a night. It had a lighted pink vacancy sign, and another sign reading CAL-INN. The view was lovely: almond groves made jagged black lines on the horizon, and I thought I smelled almonds in the air. After supper, everyone sat on the curb outside the motel. There were only two cars, besides ours and the Shibatas', in the parking lot. My brothers and I and the children from the other family played strings, cards, and *jan ken po*—the Japanese version of paper-scissors-rock. Then we sat briefly, bored, scraping and rapping our bare feet restlessly on the parking-lot concrete.

Susie Shibata and I got up to sing for everyone. I sang more on key, yet her voice had more sweetness in it, so I sat back and listened. I was singing softly along when Obāchan pushed me from my place at the curb—she'd been sitting behind me, I suppose. Ordinarily it wouldn't have occurred to me to feel indignant, because it had always been a rule that we must offer our elders our seats, and if we didn't we deserved to be forcibly removed. But Obāchan had pushed me especially hard this time. And she'd been mean to me while we were cooped up in the car. Several times she'd boxed the side of my head and told me to quiet down.

"You made me scrape my knee," I said. I held up my knee, my foot dangling in the air. "See the blood? You're in my seat and please move now."

"What did you say?" she said. She rubbed her fingers together. I could just hear the dry skin scraping.

I hesitated before answering, but I didn't want to back down. "You made me scrape my knee. Move, you witch."

She reached out and grabbed my wrist but I tried to pull it away and get up to run. She held fast, though. I wouldn't have thought she was so strong, but I couldn't get away. We called her "Pincher Obāchan" behind her back. One of her methods of punishment when we misbehaved was to smile as if she loved you with her full heart, all the while squeezing you inside the wrist. You were supposed to smile back as best you could. I have a funny picture of one of my brothers getting pinched. With that smile, he looked like a lunatic. Now, I opened my lips and pressed my teeth hard together, and tried to keep my eyes opened wide. Obāchan smiled easily back at me as she pinched. The lighting made her gums look brown, and I knew her top teeth were dentures. I was determined to outsmile her. Once, when she'd got mad at Ben and pinched him for something like fifteen minutes, he outsmiled her, and finally she broke down and patted his head and gave him a nickel. I would make her give me a nickel, too. But she didn't stop, and after a while I felt my pulse between her fingers. I thought that the vein would burst, or that my skin might fall off in her hands.

"You've got the record!" encouraged Ben. Meaning it had been more than fifteen minutes.

Obāchan seemed to pinch more tightly. "All right!" I said. She let go and I went off to sit by myself. My mother came over and ran her hand over my head. When I felt I could talk without crying, I said, "Mom, I was just sitting there. She pushed me. You saw."

"She's old," said my mother. "But I'll tell her to be less hard on you. Okay?"

"She's evil," I said. "When she smiles I see she's a devil." I sucked on my wrist.

My mother laughed. "Oh, you never even knew her during her pinching prime. I could tell you stories."

"Obāchan pinching stories!" I said. "That's the last thing I want to hear."

My father rose to go in, as did Mr. Shibata. "Seven o'clock?" said my dad. Mr. Shibata nodded. Seven was when we would start out the next day. Before he went in, my father knelt beside me and my mother. "How'd you like to sit in front with us tomorrow?"

"Okay."

"You can have the window if you want or the middle if you want," said my mother.

"Thank you," I said. But I wasn't appeased.

My father went in. My mother followed with Peter, and I followed her. I didn't want to sit outside with Obāchan.

My mother sat on the bed and leafed through a book about presidents' wives. She envied presidents' wives and liked to know what they ate and wore, liked to know the odd fact that made them human. For instance, she liked knowing that Andrew Jackson's wife married him mistakenly thinking she'd obtained a divorce from her first husband, or knowing that Mrs. Polk, who was very religious, prohibited liquor and dancing in the White House—"No wonder the Polks had no children," she would say. She'd probably inherited her interest in first ladies from Obāchan, who used to revere the Japanese emperor and his wife. "The emperor was a moron," Obāchan once said, "but he was still emperor."

My grandmother came inside; I went out.

It was always a relief when she went in for the evening, but it felt especially wonderful that night. Ben and I played tag in the back of the motel, and later we peeked into the rooms of strangers, but saw nothing. When we'd finished playing, only Mrs. Shibata and Susie still sat on the curb.

Though Obāchan always went inside early, usually when a car approached the motel office, she would come to the door and say, "Get in. What will people think with Japanese hanging around like hoodlums at night?" We would all go in, watch until the car had left, then wander out, continuing this wandering in and out until it was time for bed. But tonight, a car drove up and I waited expectantly for Obāchan's voice. When it didn't come I figured she'd gone to sleep, and I turned around, idly, to glance through the open door. I was really quite shocked to see my grand-mother, looking cadaverous in the neon, standing at the doorway silently watching the car. She came out and sat with us briefly, an event unprecedented at that hour. She talked of her life. "My memories are a string of pearls and rocks," she said. She stretched her bony hands through the air, so that I could almost see the string extended over the concrete lot. But in another minute she turned to me in one of her furies. "*I* don't know," she cried. But I didn't know what she was talking about. With all the older peo-ple I knew, even with my parents who were not so old, I occasionally saw that fierce expression as they exclaimed over something that had happened years ago, losses in a time and place as far removed from my twelve-year-old mind as the events in a schoolbook.

Later I lay on the floor under the sheets. My wrist still hurt. I couldn't sleep. I watched as my grandmother got up to go to the bathroom. Obāchan was in there for a long time, and after a while I started to hear noises like cough-ing. I got up and knocked on the bathroom door, but Obāchan didn't answer.

The door was unlocked, though. Obāchan lay in her housedress on a towel she must have placed on the floor. It was just my imagination, I realized that later, but at the time I thought she seemed to have been expecting me. She was already not of this world, and she spoke with a fury un-natural even for her. "You! Get your mother," she said. It was a hiss, a rasp, and a cracked whisper all at once. I felt cold, as if there were ghosts in the room. But it was my own body, making me cold in the warm night. I reached back and closed the door and turned to watch her again.

"Get your mother," Obāchan said. Still with fury, but, now, something else, too. The hint of a "please" in her voice.

I saw in the mirror that I was crying and shaking. I had hated my grandmother for so long.

"Get your mother." This time Obāchan sounded desperate, pleading.

She said it two more times, once with draining hope and the last time peacefully. "Get your mother," she said, with calm peaceful resignation. She closed her eyes and I left. I got under the sheets again. Dim light shone through the sheet over my head, a glow like very early morning. Sometimes, when I couldn't quite place what I was feeling, I would search through my body, from my toes up to my calves and between my legs and on up to my head. Now, my stomach hurt. I thought I heard a noise from the bathroom. Obāchan was *ready* to die, I thought. And then I felt very sleepy.

When I woke it was because Walker had found Obāchan dead on the bathroom floor. He clung to me as we stood at the door. My mother stood over her mother, horrified. My father was grim.

"She made me kill her!" I said.

"She made me kill her!" Walker echoed.

My parents just thought I was crazy.

We sent Obāchan's body to Wilcox, California, which

was where her third husband was buried, and drove there for the funeral. As I watched the casket being buried, I felt surrounded by a cool, choking mist that made me cough up phlegm and made my eyes smart and water, and I knew that Obāchan was there. But the coldness went away. I looked toward the sky, to see whether my grandmother's ghost might be floating heavenward. "No, she must have gone there," I said, pointing with my thumb toward the ground. My father gave me a disapproving look.

Peter pointed at the gravestone and the red plastic flowers we'd left. "Obāchan?" he said.

After that we headed to Los Angeles to visit relatives. On the drive down we had some of Obāchan's riches: enameled boxes and painted fans, and old journals filled with graceful Japanese writing. We had a picture of her as a beautiful woman in her twenties. As I looked at the picture I got a feeling that I get even sometimes today, that there are things I am scared to know, not mystical things—that's what I *want* to know about—but things about bad luck.

Here's the way my mother, when I was older, explained my grandmother's death. "My mother was a guilty woman— she told me once that she felt guilty about the way she treated you, and about other things from her life. My mother was also frugal. She didn't believe anything should be wasted. She gave you her boxes, her fans, her pictures, your memories of her nice walks. And that night she gave you her guilt: use it."

MARY F.
CHEN
· · · · · · · ·

Knuckles

A dog would have saved my life. Under the table, gulping
down greasy chunks of squid or duck. A bone-crunching
dog. Still, I had my sister, Jane. She ate steadily, her droopy
baby cheeks flapping in and out with each bite. After dinner, my parents would go into the living room to watch the
news. Minutes later, Jane finished eating and ran clumsily
up our long hallway after them. I could hear the bells on
her shoes as she raced the whiteness of the walls. I switched
our two bowls.

"Finished, Ma!" I smiled at Jane and flopped down in
front of my father's chair. "But Jane didn't."

A sigh and my mother bustled up the hall to check. Jane
was mildly confused, but accepting, and she ate. A few
days later the routine made my mother suspicious. She began staying in the kitchen with me until I finished. I stared
at bulging fish eyes and clutching chicken feet on the plates,
mouthing my apologies to the dead things. Did it hurt, I

wondered, when they ripped the hook out of your mouth? Did you do a funny legless dance?

One day Mama tired of my lamenting over sectioned eel and hopped up and down furiously. "Stop it! Stop it! Why are you talking to the eel?" She held the plate up to my nose. "Eat!"

On television earlier that day, the animal people had slipped into black rubber suits and sunk into the ocean. Eels waved lazily back and forth between giant rocks while the men prodded them with long poles. Suddenly one of the eels flashed out at a diver and the man grabbed his arm. They had to return to the boat.

"I don't like eel!"

"Stupid. They're a delicacy. You should be grateful. Eat!"

I held my breath.

Cecilia Grottenmyer and the other second-grade girls would laugh when they found out I had been electrocuted by an eel. All that would be left of me: ashes. My parents would keep me in a jar on the top shelf of the pantry next to the cocoa tin. On a dry, winter day, the jar would tilt during an unguarded nudge, then crash as Mama reached for the cocoa. In her confusion, Mama would drop the tin. Dust fumes, me and cocoa, everywhere until an efficient swoop of the vacuum left the floor slick again.

I gasped for breath and sucked in eel, the smell tumbling me out of my chair and back against the wall.

"No!"

She shoved a spoonful of the meat past my pressed lips,

quickly jerked out the spoon, and squeezed my lips shut. She stepped back and folded her arms. I smiled sadly at her and threw up.

After that, she left me alone in the kitchen. I became creative. I sifted through garbage until my dinner was safely at the bottom of the bag. I threw food out of our kitchen window and watched it pop like a balloon two floors down. When I felt hungry, I took the honey from the top of the refrigerator and dipped spoonfuls of fish or pork in it, careful not to let any food fall into the jar.

They must all come out.

I clenched my teeth. What if I promise to brush after every meal? Eat stuff that doesn't come in foil? The dentist smiled. He tucked in my bib and flicked on the light, sucking my thoughts into the glare.

My mother shook her head at the dentist. Nonono. I do not let my children eat candy. Her bad friends must have given her candy. I cook only things that are good for her.

I leaned away from the glaring light, but dancing green spots veiled my eyes. The spots looked like tiny floating faces, laughing and scolding. They taunted and followed my vision until I hid myself again in the yellow of the light.

"We ate rice noodles and almost nothing else for months when I arrived. All of Baba's savings paid to bring me to America." Mama was knitting in the dark, speaking to me softly as I cried. "Your grandmother always made sure that our dinner table had plenty of red-braised meats, vegetables in spicy sauces. Two kinds of soup. But I wouldn't let myself think about that then or I would have hated your baba for being poor every time I cooked noodles."

I couldn't see Mama. Her voice seemed to come from the darkness itself. I wanted to call out and tell her to turn on the light, but my mouth was still numb and clogged with blood and tears. My gums throbbed. The *click-click* of the knitting needles made the softness in her voice less scary.

Cecilia slipped in and out of my dreams. Over lunches of finger foods, we sat laughing together. We were tied for prettiest girl in class. Now we were in her ruffled pink bedroom, exchanging confidential tips on how to braid our long, golden hair. We traded clothes. Mama barged in, wearing her familiar printed housecoat and handed me shimmering, high-collared gowns of jeweled reds and purples. I touched the silk, slowly fingering the embroidered buttons. Mama was a girl again, with happy slaps of pink in her cheeks and dangling ornaments twirled into her glossy hair. She motioned for me to try on the gowns, but my arms were full of Cecilia's jeans and sweaters. Mama was floating away. Cecilia was floating away. I wanted to yell for them to wait but I had forgotten the words to say.

Mama wiped away my tears with a cool cloth and slid back into the darkness. "After a while, we were able to buy chicken once a week and I began learning to cook. In Taiwan, the servants prepared the meals."

At school I stood in line to get free lunch tickets. The white envelope marked "Grace Lin Lunch Money" remained hidden inside my jacket where my mother pinned it each Monday morning. In the lunchroom I handed my green ticket to the cashier and carried my tray to the first-grade table.

"Hey, Gracie! It's my turn to dump." Misty nudged in next to me. Her thin, black fingers scooped up the gray lumps from my plate and plopped them into paper napkins. She sauntered to the water fountain. Bending over for a drink, she quickly dropped the bundle in the trash. She glanced around before skipping back toward me.

I laughed, putting an arm around her.

"We've only got fifteen minutes left, we'd better hurry." Misty grabbed her emptied tray and headed for the Mean Lady. I followed, but a third-grader cut in front of me.

"Hold it." A huge brown hand snatched the third-grader's shoulder and pushed him into an empty seat. "That's not enough. Eat some more." The boy peered up at the black-walnut face and frantically stuffed forkfuls of mush into his mouth.

I gripped my tray and stared at Misty waving at me from the other end of the line. I shrunk under the stare of the Mean Lady and walked quickly to the dirty-forks bin.

On our way outside we passed the table where Cecilia and her friends sat. The girls pulled thermoses and neat squares of sandwiches out of bright lunch boxes. The ends of their long blond hair brushed back and forth over their food as each turned from side to side, laughing and talking. Cecilia always sat at the middle of the table. She ate foods in geometric shapes.

We followed the thick rope of children streaming past the Texaco station to Mr. Henry's. I stopped in front of the fat Italian ice man for a limie. He stared sadly into the distance as he poured the green liquid, his mustache pointing dejectedly, accusingly down at me. Grabbing the cone, I dropped a dime into his open palm. I was careful to avoid looking at the dark, glazed eyes.

Inside Mr. Henry's, we jostled and screamed along and paid for chips and twirled wands of licorice with coins carefully counted out from white envelopes. Misty leafed through comic books and slipped Hershey bars into her coat pocket. I bought peppermint, chocolate malt balls, Pixie Sticks.

I stashed leftover purchases under the love seat in the living room. For hours I would lie in the space between the furniture and the wall, slowly and slowly chewing potato chips. I listened to Jane yelling for me as chocolate melted in my mouth. My mother minced garlic while I twirled gum slowly around my fingers, stretching the orange wads into wisps.

The dentist held up a poster of a magnified set of teeth. He handed me a giant toothbrush. Show me how you brush dear show me. I swirled the toothbrush over the glossy teeth but he frowned. No dear it's up and down do it for me dear can you show me how to brush your teeth dear? I swirled the brush faster but he shook his head. No no can you do it right dear show me the way it's supposed to be. But I could only hang on to the toothbrush as it swirled in frantic circles. The dentist clucked at me and, with a black magic marker, X'ed out each tooth.

"I was very careful to buy the best food for the least amount of money. Anything that didn't have to be cold, I put in milk crates. Long strips of sticky tape around the boxes kept the cockroaches from our things."

Click-click.

I could feel my mother nodding and smiling.

"Every morning, cockroaches of all sizes were stuck on the tape. Some dead, some still moving. I threw them into the garbage and put on new tape."

The nurse finished cleaning my teeth and patted my head. Okay doctor everything is ready I'm sorry Mrs. Lin you'll have to wait outside okay. I jammed my feet against the footrest and sunk back into the green cushion, but the fat hand brought the white mask closer and closer. I shook my head and whipped my hair until the nurse grabbed my ears. The dentist slipped the mask over my nose and mouth. Thank you Nurse she'll be out soon boy she's a wild one.

I thought about Misty's black fingers and Italian ices and

not letting anyone take my teeth. The hissing of the gas sounded like shaken-up Coke bottles opened just a little.

I used to ask what we were having for dinner. "Shaun chiao tu tzu and hai dai hua sheng pai ku tang." Was it a special occasion? My stomach snarled in approval until I realized we were having pork stomach and kelp-and-peanut soup. I wondered vaguely if Mama was trying to trick me. How could something that sounded as good as "Chao ku feng dan" be chicken liver?

There was never new food. The same dishes reappeared week after week. The amount, the smell, the seasonings, the colors, never changing. Mama must have dug under-ground vats while I was at school, filling them with day-long-made pots of stuff. Filling and filling until there would always be more to spoon out year after year. Filling until the brown and gold and green sauces hiding animal parts spilled out over the edges of the vats and flowed out into the basement. Shredded pork with sweet bean paste and stuffed glutinous duck with brown sauce spread across the floor. Crispy chicken legs crept up the walls. Sharks' fin soup seeped into the living room and into our bedrooms, into our clothes and noses. Nagging at our brains day and night. At school everyone knew what I ate because my clothes smelled and had turned into the familiar browns and golds and greens.

Even the ceiling was discolored. My mother stood for hours in front of the sink and stove, chopping and frying and not throwing anything away. She made dinners from one animal: ribs floating in soup and tongues cleverly sliced and sauced to look like steak. Great balls of steam leaped from popping vegetables and hovered over her head like angry genies until, with a wave of her apron, they vanished. Years of wrestling smelly fish and hot oil had left a huge brown splotch on the ceiling above the stove. During the winter's darkness I crept up the hall to watch Mama cooking under a single dull light. The brown stain looked black in the dimness and the hot vapors flew up and into their depths. I shivered at the thought of severed chicken and pig souls trying to find their way to heaven to piece themselves together again.

I was relieved when we moved. I raced through our new house, happy to see and touch the unblemished walls. I rolled on the new carpeting, letting the dust go up my nose and cling to my hair. I shut myself in the closet to sit with the stillness and trapped air.

Pushing the furniture away from the walls, I crawled into the space. Flicking up the back skirt of the love seat, I reached up and unpinned bags of chocolate. I ripped the bags open and smelled the drowsy sweetness. One by one, the chunks melted in my mouth and oozed down my throat.

My mother went straight to work cleaning, slicing and cooking. Under the new fluorescent light, she raised her spatula and wooden chopsticks, plunging them down to stir and turn the crackling food. Oil snapped out at her, but again and again, her hands forged into the pans. The screaming of the frying foods was tamer on the new electric stove, but my mother tricked the meats and vegetables into the familiar flavors. Within minutes, the smell had found us.

Somebody turned on a light in the hallway and a little brightness pushed in under the crack of my door. I could see the silhouette of my mother's feet, and I tried to imagine the dried, callused toes snug in sapphire slippers trimmed in pearl. The girlhood slippers Mama stored, wrapped in plastic, in her drawer.

My mother shifted in her chair and continued knitting. The clicking was becoming steadier as her hands learned to see in the dark.

"When you were born, I was already a good cook. Your baba was getting fat and friends came to visit. I never bought baby food. You ate what Baba and I ate. I chewed a mouthful of food until it was soft and smooth, then fed it to you. You were always so happy to eat. By the time you were two, you could use chopsticks and eat by yourself." Her sigh filled the room.

One Monday night my parents promised us dinner at Lenny's Pizza & Subs on the corner. Jane and I boasted about who was hungrier and how much could we eat and worried about do we have enough money. It was our first dinner out.

"Can we help you order?"

My father carefully picked us off his arm and pushed us toward the tables. "Go sit down, I will order."

Jane ran to a corner booth, but I dragged her toward a center table. A group of older girls from school sat a few seats away. I yawned loudly and looked bored, but watched the girls' reflection carefully in the window.

"Here we are. I hope you're hungry."

My father proudly passed out small cartons of milk and one straw each. He tucked a napkin under his chin and waited expectantly. My mother opened her bag, taking out chopsticks and round, metal tins. She grinned broadly and pulled the lids off the containers, releasing swirls of steam. I felt the other girls' eyes staring at our colorful dinner and knew that I would never be asked to sit at their table.

"I hope you children are hungry. This is a special occasion so I made a lot." My mother chewed happily and passed me a napkin.

I watched the food churning in her mouth; her blunt fingers reached in to loosen chunks of food stuck between her teeth. Mama brought out a small bag from under the table. "A special surprise for this special occasion." She pulled out neat rectangles of cherry pie wrapped in shiny cardboard. "The sign says these are very good. Here." She placed one in front of each of us.

I put mine over the metal tin and peered at the girls' reflection through my bangs. They were sharing milkshakes and pulling pepperoni off their pizza. My mother was eating cherry pie with her chopsticks. She spoke loudly in Taiwanese, proclaiming the blandness of American food and the cleanliness of some public rest rooms.

Why are you doing this to me, I grumbled in my cheeks. Everyone's going to know now.

"Huh? What did you say?" Mama peered suspiciously at me. "Speak louder."

I want to go home. Everybody's looking at us. I raised my voice but kept it in my throat. I want pepperoni, too.

"Huh?"

I bit into my cherry pie and screamed, "This isn't eating out! What do you mean this is eating out? This is worse than eating at home! If we have to eat this stuff, do we have to do it where everyone can see?" I pinched Jane until she screamed. "See, Jane wants to go, too!"

The girls at the other table had stopped eating to stare at me. I sat down. My father sighed and popped the last of his pie into his mouth. Mama slapped some pennies in front of me and continued eating. "Want everything? Want peeza? Here. You get it."

The girls were leaving. I ran to the bathroom and threw the coins into the toilet.

My mother was standing by the dentist again. She frowned at the black X's on the chart and asked if she could use some of the sleeping gas. She pulled a huge wok out of her bag and made a stove out of the dentist's equipment. She put my teeth into the pan and started stirring. But the

dentist said he wasn't hungry. My mother told him he had
to eat anyway.

Breakfasts were soothing after anxious dinners. I liked the
baldness of toast and the sogginess of cereal. I knew where
to find the butter and the stainless-steel knives. One morning a fat cockroach the size of my nose fell from the ceiling
into my father's coffee. It didn't die. Fluttering and fluttering, its blackness made it invisible except for the dimples of
its feet.

The soreness in my neck made me realize that I was straining to hear my mother. She dropped her words softly as if
knitting them into a sweater to keep herself warm. I was
leaning out toward the clicking of her needles.

"I don't understand why you stopped liking my food."
Mama stopped knitting.

The silence loosened the tethers of time. I could feel the
dull ache in my mouth but couldn't be sure whether my
imagination was still dancing with white masks. Slowly the
clicking began again.

"Later, when Jane was born, I fed her the same way I fed
you and she became happy. Fat. The other mothers were
jealous at the way she could eat." Mama laughed. "She ate
more than other children twice her age."

My head snapped back and forth as the Mean Lady shook
me. Not enough not enough. I wanted to tell her to stop,
but I couldn't find her face beneath the brown creases and

thick glasses. I can't eat anymore, I couldn't tell her. All my teeth are gone. Quiet quiet, a fat man said. Girls with no teeth cannot have special ice.

Far away, someone chanted, "Wakeupwakeupwakeup."

"Not you. No. Not my firstborn. So picky now. Everything is 'Yucky' and you're always 'Not hungry.' To me, everything is delicious after I work many hours making dinner. When I sit down, the food tastes good. I eat until I am full."

My body was absorbing the numbness of my mouth and pushing the pain outward. I could feel the cavities eating away teeth that weren't there anymore. The throbbing of my gums pulsed in time with the *click-click* of my mother's needles.

"Just look at your baba. He eats and eats and is happy. He's quiet because he likes his life. It's a good life with family, job, house, food, and clothes."

I pictured the man who sat like a boulder to eat with us once a week. Fourteen hours a day, six days a week, in a Chinatown rice shop he worked. The man who only wanted to sleep and be left alone.

I carefully picked out tendons and gooey things, but my mother told me that only Indians eat with their fingers and to just swallow the whole thing.

"Just because you like it doesn't mean I do." I winced at the rubbery pig knuckles.

"You children just don't know what's good." She placed another helping in my bowl. "When I was young, my mother made pig knuckles and porridge to warm us up in the winter. We had to walk seven kilometers to school. Nothing was better for keeping us warm."

"How come Jane got a smaller piece than me?" I held my knuckles against hers.

"Stupid. In Taiwan, everyone would be fighting for the biggest pieces, and you're complaining because I gave you a big piece? You don't know." She tapped my bowl with her chopsticks, motioning for me to eat.

"Be quiet!" my father said. "Dinnertime is supposed to be peaceful."

I stared at the rice dangling from his ragged mustache.

"Hurry up." My mother tapped my bowl.

I buried the knuckles under the rice and stabbed them, making my chopsticks stand straight up.

"I can't eat my rice. I'm full."

Mama's hand swept over my ear, cheek, nose. "Don't do that!" She jerked my chopsticks up, pork knuckles and all, with rice flying in a snowy arch, and placed the utensils on the table.

"Do what?" I rubbed my cheek and picked up the scattered rice on the table, squishing the ones on the floor with my toes.

She pulled off a huge strip of meat and chewed in gulping breaths. "Don't stick your chopsticks up like that!"

"That's why you hit me?" I silently pounded the table.

"What's wrong with that anyway? I was resting my chopsticks." I considered putting them back up.

"Chopsticks up in food are offerings for dead people." She pried the knuckles off my sticks and placed the utensils across my bowl. "Keep them like this when you're not eating. Who taught you to put them up? My mother would have said, 'You want to give your food to the dead, then we will give it to the dead!' and I would go hungry. How come you do things like that? You children think you're so great."

I lifted my tongue but all I could feel was soggy gauze. Somehow I thought I was a hero. I had undergone something terrible, something that hurt. I had blood on my clothes.

Mama pulled out the soaked wads of gauze and stuffed fresh rolls in. I wanted her to look at my blood and see me sweating with pain. I wanted her to hear how I didn't cry.

"Eat."

I pulled the knuckles off my chopsticks and plopped them into my bowl. I ate my rice one by one, chewing and swallowing each grain before continuing. Soon everyone wandered into the living room and I was alone. Taking careful aim, I speared the knuckles with my chopsticks, but the huge blocks, with no rice packed around them, kept tipping over. I pushed up the window screen and tossed the knuckles out.

"I should make you go outside and pick that up." My mother stood in the doorway, pulling back a strand of hair and pushing it behind her ear. "I spend hours cooking for you and you throw food out the window?"

I put my bowl in the sink. Once, she made me stand in a corner for six hours because I forgot to practice playing the piano. "Sorry. I'll go get it."

She picked up her stained apron and snapped it loudly in the air. "No. What's the use? Will you eat it? Of course not. You don't care how much time I spend preparing the food. You'll flush it down the toilet. You'll throw it in the closet. You're a very mean girl."

As Mama gestured wildly, I noticed the numerous nicks and spots of oil burns on her hands.

"You never appreciate anything." She began pacing, tossing her head like a gored bull. "I work so hard to make dinner. If we lived in Taiwan, we would have maids and cooks and I could sit in the garden fanning myself all day and not getting my clothes dirty. I could wear my beautiful gowns again. Every color. All silk." She walked faster. "No more cooking. Like when I was a girl. My father rang a bell and the servants put the food on the table. He rang another bell and everyone came to eat. A feast every night. We finished everything. Even during poor harvests, our family always had a lot. We ate and ate."

I picked a grain of rice off the floor.

She stopped walking and glared at me. Her eyes shone. "All you do is complain! I didn't come to this country to be a servant to my own children! I should have stayed in Taiwan!"

❀

Mama led me from the dentist's office and stretched me out across the backseat of our car. Baba sat quietly behind the steering wheel, turning to smile. My face was an over-stuffed sack of cotton and blood. One hand clutched a small cloth doll. It was ugly with orange yarn hair and limp arms, but it had been enough to lure me into the dentist's chair. I wasn't a hero. I was hungry and humiliated. Spots of color had followed me out of the dental office.

We drove thousands of miles to get home. The whistle of wind from a cracked window blew me back to fight the charm of white masks in a sterile room. The light was an orange cinnamon fireball. The white paper cups were filled with strawberry syrup. A seat belt kept me strapped to the padded chair, bound my hands. The mask stilled my shrieks. In the seats next to me, Cecilia was having her teeth polished and Misty was feeding pig knuckles to the Mean Lady. Chinese sauces came up a tube, into the mask and down my throat. The light went out and everything was gone except the tightening mask. I was choking. My stomach felt like the blown-out throat of a bullfrog, but the sauces kept pouring into me. Choking me in spiciness. Sesame oil thickening my throat. Ginger roots burning my tongue. The distant tastes mingling with the blood from my gums.

A hand brought sudden air and the tightness lifted. A cool cloth smoothed away sweat and tears, I could open my eyes. The bitter, soothing taste of tea trickled down my throat, forcing the passage open and washing down the thickness. My mother tilted the cup again and waited for me to swallow.

Fortune Teller

Andy hated it when someone disturbed his nap, especially an after-school nap (because according to him, it was much healthier than vitamins and milk), but this particular Friday, he had overslept. So he wasn't irritated at all when his sister Hoa squeezed his fat cheek and stretched it and let it go and the piece of fat snapped back at his face like a rubber band and woke him up. When this usually happened, Andy would mumble, "May the fat Budda fart at whoever just did that." And then he'd pull the blanket over his head and go back to sleep. His two younger sisters, Hoa and Phương, loved to bug him because Andy was their only brother, and also, he had been the only male in the house until their father had come over from Vietnam eight months ago. But tonight when Hoa woke Andy up, he immediately tossed the blanket off his body and rolled over on his elbows and looked at the alarm clock by his bed.

"Five after nine," said Andy before looking at Hoa. "Little Bugar, you've saved my life."

Little Hoa giggled, showing tiny crooked teeth. "*Mẹ* called you," she said.

Andy wasn't listening. He jumped off his bed and walked to his open closet. He immediately dug through the rack of hanging shirts and jackets, a pile of folded sweaters on the top shelf, and then the basket of dirty clothes on the floor. Finally, he pulled out a white dress shirt under the sweaty socks. Andy sniffed the shirt. "Oh man, that sucks," he said.

"You're going somewhere?" asked Hoa.

"Big Brother here is going to a birthday party."

"Whose birthday?"

"Dan. You don't know him."

"Can I come?"

Andy found his favorite baggy jeans to match the white shirt. "No. Only beautiful people can come," he said, thinking of Jennifer.

"I'm beautiful," said Hoa, and then she placed one hand by her waist and the other under her chin. "See!"

"No, you're not. Look at that big mole on your neck. Looks like a big fly that flew and crashed onto your neck and stuck there."

"No, no, no. You're wrong. *Bố* said that I'm beautiful and that I'm going to be rich because I have this mole."

"Oh?" *Bố*, his father, was a part-time fortune teller. In the daytime, he was a gardener, but at night he read people's fortunes at Duyen's Restaurant. He practiced astrology best, but he could also read cards, palms, and even face features. So if there was anything to say about an ugly mole, *Bố* would know. "That black thing is going to make you rich, hah? We'll see about that. Anyway, get out! I need to change."

Andy pushed Hoa out of his room. Before he could close the door, Hoa said, "Wait. *Mẹ* wants you."

"Yeah?"

"Yes. Why you think I woke you up?"

"Really? What does mother want? I know. She wants me to help her wrap *bánh trứng*, right?"

"I don't know. I'm not a fortune teller like *Bố*. Come out and ask her yourself." And then Hoa turned her head with her chin up and walked away.

"Tell *Mẹ* that I'll be out in a minute."

Andy closed the door. He pulled out the iron and ironing board from under his bed. He ironed his jeans first and made sure there were no wrinkles left around the jeans' back pockets. He didn't want Jennifer to think that he was sloppy, and worse, to think that he had a flat butt. He ironed the white shirt next. It had been in the dirty laundry basket for some time, but that was no problem. Andy added some water to the iron and turned on the steam. He pressed and pressed, and the steam sizzled on his shirt and evaporated some of the odor. When he finished ironing, the long-sleeved shirt looked whiter than before.

He suddenly remembered that he hadn't showered. After

school he had played basketball with his friends until six. When he came home, he dropped dead right away on his bed. Then Hoa squeezed his cheek and woke him up. Now it was already nine fifteen. Dan had told Andy that his birthday party was at eight. But Dan was Vietnamese, so eight meant nine. And Andy hoped to get there by ten; that was when the party would start happening anyway.

Rushing to the bathroom, he wet a towel and wiped off his face and neck. Then he tilted his head into the sink and turned on the faucet and let the warm water run over his hair. After drying his hair, he applied mousse and streaked it back the fast-slicky style. His body still felt moist and sticky. But it didn't matter. At the party he'd ask Jennifer to dance, and then he'd be all sweaty and sticky anyway.

Andy walked back to his room. Standing in front of the mirror on the closet door, he stripped down to his briefs and checked himself out. He was pretty big for a sixteen-year-old Vietnamese.

As he put on his jeans and shirt, he wondered what Jennifer would wear tonight. He liked her style. In school, she usually wore jeans, a T-shirt, and leather shoes like everyone else, but somehow she just looked better. Her jeans weren't just jeans; they were loose and long to her heel and flared out at the end, almost like bell-bottoms. Her shirt wasn't white, but off-white, beige, gray, khaki, and large enough to be trendy but small enough to show off her slender body. And once in a while she'd wear a V neck, and her smooth collar bones would shine in the sun during lunch. And she had short hair like a boy, but she walked like no boys. And sometimes on a free-spirit day, Jennifer would wear a long cotton dress that would run down to her ankles and seem to cover her entire body, and Andy's entire world as well because he'd see nothing else but her face and her dress. She could be so sexy, mysteriously sexy.

Jennifer was a junior like Andy, but it was only her first year at Silver Creek. Her family had moved down to San Jose from Orange County. And Andy was fortunate to have the same English class with Jennifer. The fact that the class was English III spoke something for itself. Juniors were supposed to be at English III level. But Andy had a heavy accent and his grammar was bad, so he belonged in English II. Jennifer, on the other hand, hardly had any accent and her essays were excellent. Andy told Jennifer many times that she belonged in English III or even English III Honor, but Jennifer just shrugged her shoulders and said that she didn't want to read more Shakespeare.

He liked her. He liked her ever since the first day of his junior year. And because she talked to him, even though it was just casual talk, and talked to him in English he liked her even more. And once in a while she'd throw in a few Vietnamese words, like *cà trớn*, *lấu cà*, or *thằng hề* with her northern accent to describe his clowning behavior, and that drove him *phê*—happily nuts. In class he sat several rows away from her, and several months into the second year Mrs. Becker shuffled the students around for variety, and he sat even farther away from her. But his feelings for her never faded. Actually, he liked that long-distance view of her, where he got to see everything around her. To him, the world revolved around her, around her oval face, around her white ankles.

There were many occasions when Andy wanted to ask Jennifer out. He wanted to ask her to go to the Winter Ball, a very formal dance, but he thought maybe he should let her know him better before asking her out on such a big date. He wanted to ask her to go watch a wrestling match after school because his friend was on the team, but then he was afraid that she'd fall in love with one of those boys. And then he got her number from a girlfriend of a friend of a friend, so on New Year's Day he called her up to see if she wanted to take a walk through the Japanese Garden and perhaps they'd stand on the little wooden red bridge and look down at those colorful fish in the pond and maybe she'd let him hold her hand, but a man answered the phone and Andy hung up. The closest he ever got to be with her was when she forgot to bring *A Separate Peace* to read aloud in class; Andy hopped across five rows of desks to offer her his book. And in that brief ten minutes when she was reading to the class in her almost perfect English, Andy was beside her, holding his breath. Then when the class gathered close to the TV to watch *Romeo and Juliet,* he sat in a desk behind her. And he leaned forward to smell her hair but then all of a sudden his nose bled. And in the end of the movie, after both Romeo and Juliet had died, Jennifer suddenly giggled and said to her girlfriend, "How corny. Love like that would never happen in real life."

Of course love like that could happen.

Andy waited and waited. He predicted that the right moment would eventually come. And he was right. The opportunity finally came last week, when Dan passed out invitations to his birthday party. Jennifer and Andy both got one. Andy saw his chance on a piece of paper, and he held it tight between his fingers.

Today, after class, Andy had caught up with Jennifer to make sure.

"Are you coming to Dan's party tonight?" he asked her.

"Oh, I think so, but I haven't got him a gift yet," she said. "How about you?"

"Yeah . . . I just want to see . . . if you need a ride there?"

"Well, I think my sister will take me there. But maybe you can give me a lift home."

"Oh, sure. No problem."

"Okay, so I'll see you there," said Jennifer.

"Yeah!"

And Jennifer turned away to walk to her next class, but after a few steps she turned back.

"Oh, Andy. Do you know what Dan likes?"

Andy was looking at her white ankles. "Umm . . . socks? White socks?"

"Oh?" Jennifer nodded, and then she disappeared down the hallway.

And now Andy stood in front of the mirror and checked to see if his white shirt was tucked in evenly. He took out the Polo in his drawer and tapped some on his neck and on the collar, shoulders, and arms of his shirt. He was prepared to ask Jennifer to slow-dance. And if everything worked out, and he could tell if everything worked out or not by the way she'd look at him when he was slow-dancing with her, he'd tell her everything. He'd pour his soul out during that slow song, and even more when he gave her a ride home.

He walked out of his room and to the kitchen. His mother was sitting on the floor, wrapping *bánh trưng*, rice cake. Phương was next to her mother, drying the large banana leaves with a towel. Hoa, who was beside Phương, took the dried leaves from her twin sister and cut the outer veins with a scissor. There were several plastic buckets in front of them: buckets of soaked sweet rice, a bucket of steamed crushed mung beans, and a bucket of sliced salted pork. There wasn't room left on the floor even to walk to the refrigerator.

"*Mẹ*, you called me?" asked Andy.

"*Ừ.*" His mother glanced up. "Where are you planning to go that requires so much cologne?"

"Brother Andy, help us," said Phương.

"Yes. Stay home and help us," joined Hoa.

His mother took some banana leaves and cut them into long strips and placed them neatly inside the small wooden frame resting on the tile floor. She poured one bowl of sweet rice inside and spread it evenly to cover the bottom sides. This was the outer layer of *bánh trửng*. Next she poured a smaller bowl of yellow mung beans inside to make the second layer. Three slices of thick salted pork were placed in the center. Then came a bowl of mung beans again, and a bowl of sweet rice after that to complete the filling. She folded the banana leaves and wrapped the cake. With her palms she pressed down hard before pulling out the frame. She wrapped a final layer of aluminum foil around the cakes to protect the leaves from breaking after ten hours of boiling. The last touch was red nylon string tightened around each cake. Each one looked like a wrapped gift box.

Andy counted eighteen wrapped *bánh trửng*. His mother was planning to wrap forty this year, ten more than last year because she just bought a bigger aluminum trash can, and according to Mrs. Châu, her lady friend, that trash can could fit up to forty-six *bánh trửng*.

"*Mẹ*, I know that you want me to help you, but remember last year? I wrapped ten cakes for you, and I didn't press down hard enough so they were soft and loose after we boiled them. When you gave them to your friends, they said that you wrapped with such *light hands*. See, *Mẹ*? I made you *lose face* last year. And surely I don't want it to happen again this year. So I think that it's best if I don't wrap." Andy thought about what he had just said and smiled. He was amazed at what he could come up with sometimes.

His mother continued wrapping at a steady pace. "All right, mister. Stop talking around the world. Where do you want to go tonight?"

"My friend Dan invited me to his birthday party. Can I go, *Mẹ*?"

"Vietnamese don't celebrate birthdays," said his mother. "Maybe the rich families that lived with the French in the old days did. But even then, only girls would celebrate birthdays, not boys."

"Yeah!" agreed Hoa and Phương.

"You two be quiet. *Mẹ*, it's America. Everybody celebrates everything here. Christmas, New Year's, Mother's Day, Father's Day, birthdays—and we're at an advantage. We celebrate their holidays in addition to ours. See, that's why you're wrapping *bánh trưng*, because in a few days, we're going to celebrate *Tết*, our own New Year."

"We don't celebrate Christmas. We're Buddhists."

"Yes, you're right. But then we can use those days off from school and work," paused Andy. "*Mẹ*, does that mean I can go?"

"*Ừ*, but you have to do one thing for me first."

"What is it, *Mẹ*?"

"I cooked some *xôi*. So on your way, bring some to *Bố*."

"*Mẹ*, it's late. Who would eat *xôi* at this hour?"

"If it's not too late to go out, then it's not too late to eat."

He quickly grabbed the plate of *xôi* and rushed out the kitchen.

"Brother Andy, what time will you be home?" asked Phương.

"Why, you little . . ." Then Andy met his mother's eyes. "Twelve."

"You mean one. All right, but if you don't come home by then, then you're going to *know my hand*." His mother laughed. "Son, come home early tonight so you can help *Bố* cook the cakes."

Everything his mother did or said had to relate to his father in some way. Perhaps she was trying to make up for all those years while his father was away imprisoned in reeducation camp. And food would certainly help.

Andy nodded. He put on his shoes. Then he walked out of the house to his '82 Sentra. As he turned on the engine, he checked the time. It was nine forty-three. Pushing it, he'd reach Duyen's at about nine-fifty. Then he'd end up at the party at about ten or ten-ten at the latest. Good. Everything was still on schedule.

As he drove, he cleaned his car. He threw everything in the backseat. Jennifer would sit next to him later, so he didn't want anything to be in between them. He was glad that he had his own car, and he was sure that Jennifer would be impressed too. He had worked very hard last summer, scraping off all the gum that stuck under the desks at his school. And with his savings, he bought the Sentra. The car even had a stereo, not a very powerful one, but it was decent. Tonight he didn't want to give any of his friends a ride, because he wanted to be alone with Jennifer when he gave her a lift home. Andy picked out his favorite tape and rewound it to a romantic slow song. He'd play it later for her.

How could anybody eat *xôi*? It was tasteless. There were different kinds of *xôi*, but the one that Andy was looking at was just a plain mixture of sweet rice and yellow mung beans. You'd put them in a special pot and steam them. And you'd use your fingers to pick them up in a chunk and put it in your mouth. But how could anyone swallow that chunk down? The sweet rice was not sweet; it was sticky, and it would stick to your throat. Andy thought it was impossible for him to eat *xôi* unless he had a can of Coke to gulp it down.

But his mother didn't make *xôi* for him or his sisters. His mother knew too well that her children didn't like to eat traditional food. "Peasant's food," they'd call it. His mother made *xôi* for herself, and for her husband, and she'd offer it to her parents and her friends if they were sitting in her house. She had grown up with that kind of food as Andy had grown up with Coke. She had washed and mixed the rice and beans with her own hands and the rice and beans had fallen in love with her touch. And after she had cooked them, she'd pick them up in chunks with her fingers, and the rice and beans would stick to her fingers and refuse to leave her. She appreciated the rice and beans, and they loved her back and allowed her to taste their sweetness. But to a boy like Andy, *xôi* was tasteless, like air.

And *Tết* was coming in a couple of days, so Andy's

mother had prepared many traditional foods. It was probably the busiest time of the year for her in America. She was preparing *bánh trừng,* her specialty. She had made the special ham with pork skins and ears, and whole black peppers. She was soaking several buckets of rice at home to make different kinds of *xôi*—red, yellow, white, and black, depending on the beans. She was defrosting quails, which she'd spice and grill on New Year's Day. And there were other preparations, other necessary items. She bought a large aluminum trash can and had to make sure that it didn't leak. Tonight when Andy came home, he and his father would place all the *bánh trừng* in the new trash can, add water, start a fire, and boil the cakes for ten hours. She bought red watermelon seeds, an assortment of dried sweets, rich herbal tea, red wines that she wrapped in clear red wrappers, and red money envelopes. She asked her husband to cut several peach, plum, and apple branches from the backyard and place them in large vases to decorate the living room. She told Andy to buy several decks of cards and a set of *bầu cua cá cọp* so friends and relatives could play when they come over to visit. Andy also bought red firecrackers at a Vietnamese store. He had no fear of lighting them in front of the house door on New Year's Day since most of his neighbors were also Vietnamese, and they wouldn't get scared and call for a fire truck. But most importantly, his mother directed the family to clean the house before New Year's Day because it was bad luck to clean the house afterward. So Andy got rid of all the spider webs in the corners and he cleaned the windows. His father gathered all his astrology books and put them away. And Hoa and Phương vacuumed the house.

Tết was special. There was so much to prepare. There was no ten-to-one countdown, the spraying of champagne, a kiss with whomever, and then an abrupt halt. *Tết* was about making special dishes that took days. The house had to be decorated with flowers and many other colorful objects. And when *Tết* finally came, they lit red firecrackers to drive away bad spirits, and picked out a person with a successful year to enter the house first to bring in good luck for the entire new year to come. They shared foods and luck by giving out red money envelopes to the kids, and visiting friends and relatives and sending gifts and well wishes to everyone. The celebration would last for ten days. And why not? They'd worked hard all year. So it was only fair to not do anything for ten days, except to receive good-luck money, chew watermelon seeds, try different sweets with tea, eat *bánh trừng* with ham and pickles, and eat more *bánh trừng* with ham and pickles, and then lose all your good-luck money in gambling with your friends and relatives, but then you could always just talk and eat and hide your money for other things.

But Andy tried not to think about *Tết*. Tonight his preparations were all for Jennifer. He had prepared to look nice and smell good. He had practiced his dance steps, including the cha-cha-cha, before the mirror. He had rehearsed what to say when he'd slow-dance with her and when he'd give her a ride home. He had prepared to take the hints from her eyes saying, "Yes, Andy. I feel the same way as you. And yes, you can kiss me now." He had prepared for all these things and more. All he had left to do was to show up for the birthday party.

Andy reached Duyen's at nine-fifty-two. He parked his car and walked inside the restaurant, holding the plate of *xôi* with one hand. The place was rather lively. Most of the tables were occupied by men who looked like they could use a bath and some sleep. But they probably decided to leave their wives and children home after work and come here with their buddies to *nhậu nhẹt*: drink beers, chat noisily about anything from women to soccer to democracy, and eat the famous seven-beef courses and fish salad.

An electric toy train was making its hourly run in the restaurant that was decorated to look like a Vietnamese village. All the tables and chairs were made of bamboolike materials. There was a hut with a roof made of large palm leaves. The large train ran around the roof of the hut. About every hour, the train would make its trip around the hut and toot its whistle. And now, standing at the cashier, Mr. Son was staring at his long-running train, and smiling at its cute sound like a little kid, as if he were actually in the train, riding around the countryside of his old country, hoping to reach home soon.

Andy's father was in his usual corner table, talking to a woman about his age. Andy walked toward them. He just wanted to drop the plate on the table and then go. But his father was leaning all over the table, scribbling words on a piece of paper that had square diagrams. Andy didn't want to be rude, so he just stood there beside them.

The woman watched Andy's father intensively. Three lines of wrinkles ran across her forehead. In place of her missing eyebrows, which she perhaps had plucked off, there were two sharp black lines. Another dark blue line curved beneath each eye. And in the yellow light, her well-powdered high cheek bones brightened while her short round nose darkened. And her lips, such thin and short lips, tightened to form a crimson, diamond shape.

But Andy's father looked even more intense than the woman. He wore large square glasses. He had small eyes, and even smaller now that he was squinting. His nose was large and broad and became wider as he inhaled. His lips had no color and almost disappeared into his dark face. There was a black mole on his cheek, but Andy didn't know what it meant. And his father's hair was long and was cut into a "staircase" style by his mother so that the hair covered both ears.

His father was scribbling really fast. He wrote down Vietnamese words, most of them unreadable, and he circled and circled them and drew lines to connect the circles. He also jotted down numbers, representing years and months and something else, and he put a box around them. He sketched weird symbols in the rectangular diagrams. Written in the left upper corner of the paper was the woman's birthday and what time she was born, and in the upper right corner was her animal sign, *tý*, the rat.

"*Bố*," called Andy. He couldn't wait any longer.

His father looked up. He saw the plate of *xôi* in Andy's hand, and he smiled. He pulled out an empty chair beside him.

"Son, sit down here and wait for *Bố* a little bit." Then Andy's father turned to the woman. "This is my son, my only son."

"He's so big," said the woman.

"Son, greet Mrs. Thanh."

Andy greeted her quickly, and then he turned to his father. He wanted to tell his father that it was nine fifty-seven and he really had to run off. But his father had turned all his attention to Mrs. Thanh and the piece of paper on the table. So Andy had no choice but to sit down. He rested the plate of *xôi* on his lap. And the plate was bouncing in his lap because his right leg was shaking impatiently.

"Yes. I had checked again. This coming year definitely seems very bad for you. I advise you not to do such big business. I see more losses than profits." Andy's father spoke clearly and precisely.

"Are you sure? Can you explain again why that is so?" asked Mrs. Thanh.

"Everybody has good years and bad years, depending on his or her elements. The year of the dog is a bad year for you. Let me repeat some of the things that you should watch out for this year." His father looked directly into Mrs. Thanh's eyes. "Don't drive anywhere too far. You may get into a terrible car accident. Someone in your family is in very poor health and could die if not cared for immediately. And it looks like you're planning to do business with a friend. Am I right?"

"Oh, Lord. Yes, yes."

"You can correct me if I say something incorrect."

"No, no. What you said makes very good sense." Mrs. Thanh pointed her hand to a man in a blue suit, sitting by himself a couple of tables away. His legs were crossed. And he was smoking and drinking ice coffee.

"That's my husband," said Mrs. Thanh. "He drives me everywhere. But he drives recklessly. Every time he changes from one lane to another lane, he makes me crazy. We were planning to drive to Reno. But maybe we shouldn't. Oh, and my mother-in-law, she has diabetes. She's very weak. We take her to the doctor all the time, but I don't know if she's getting any better. And yes, I was planning to put in money to open a nail shop with this woman. But I don't know if the location is good or not."

"Hmmm. Very interesting," said Andy's father. And then he took a deep breath.

Andy took a deep breath also. He wondered how much more of this fortune telling he had to listen to. If he didn't get out of this restaurant and go to the party soon, he was going to have a really bad coming year. Indeed, another year of waiting to get another chance to be with Jennifer.

"I have to go. My husband doesn't like waiting around." said Mrs. Thanh. She pulled out her purse and opened it.

"One last thing," said Andy's father. "If you still decide to do business this year anyway, then do it by yourself. Don't share with a partner. You're an intelligent woman, but you're too honest. Your partner would be jealous and cause you harm."

"Oh, yes, yes. My husband said that I'm too straightforward. I say everything. Don't hold anything back. Not good for business. Yes, yes. Thank you very much." Mrs. Thanh handed Andy's father a twenty-dollar bill. Then she looked at Andy and asked, "Will your son here follow your profession?"

"Him? He has lived in America for too long. He doesn't believe in these things," said Andy's father.

"Neither does my husband."

Mrs. Thanh sighed and stood up. She was about to leave—the moment Andy had been waiting for—but then she turned back and asked Andy's father, "What you just said, how much of it do you think was correct?"

"If I said ten things, then at least nine are correct. But most important is that I must believe in what I say, not hold anything back. You see that I tend to say more negative than positive things. I'm not like other fortune tellers, who tell you what you want to hear."

"But you said things that are so scary."

"But that is the fortune. There's good and bad, but usually more bad than good for a common person. You need to know both."

"Hmmm. How long have you been reading fortunes?" Mrs. Thanh just wouldn't leave.

"Here in America, not too long. I've been here less than a year. But in Vietnam, ever since I was a kid. I was gifted, you see. And when I went to the army, I read for all the soldiers in my unit. There I also learned to read palms, facial features, and cards. But after '75 we lost the war, so I took off my uniform and hid. You see, I didn't want to go to reeducation camp. I hid in Đà Lạt, and I read fortunes for a living. Oh, I was real *big* there. If you don't believe me, when you go back to visit Vietnam, stop by Đà Lạt and asked for Mr. Sang—the Young Fortune Teller, they'd know. Really. I was *big* and young. And then I got married, and my wife had three kids, this boy, and two younger girls, twins. Things were going really well. But then somebody leaked. And *tụi cán bộ* came. They said that I was once a traitor and now still a traitor because I'd read people's fortunes and if they asked, I'd tell them which days were good to take the boat journey. It was true. I did do that, but I didn't deserve to be arrested. Without my predictions, those days would still be good since they were already determined. But they said that I was corrupted and they put me in the reeducation camp anyway. For seven years! Can you believe that?"

"Seven years for being a fortune teller?"

When Andy's father finished telling his story, it was ten twelve. It had taken his father almost fifteen minutes to capture his life and relive the seven years of reeducation camp and dramatize the lonely nine years of separation from his family. It had taken him fifteen minutes to summarize all his good and bad fortunes. But time could be compressed in words. And time itself was a fortune.

Mrs. Thanh finally left. She walked out of the restaurant, holding her husband's elbow. She was a tough customer. She asked everything twice and she even wanted to know the fortune teller's background. But she was generous. She gave Andy's father twenty dollars. But Mrs. Thanh seemed satisfied. She'd spread the word around.

Andy stood up. He placed the *xôi* on the table. He couldn't believe that it had taken him almost twenty minutes to do this.

"*Bố, Mẹ* wanted me to deliver this," said Andy.

His father smiled. He took the clear wrapper off. "If someone brought me this in reeducation camp, oh how happy I would have been."

Andy made an effort to smile. He tried to understand what his father meant, but really, he couldn't. Of course Andy felt bad about his father's bad fortune, and he sure missed his father during the years of his absence. But why would his father want to eat *xôi* in such a terrible situation? How could his father possibly swallow *xôi* down?

"*Bố,* I have to go," said Andy.

"Where are you going? Stay here and eat *xôi* with me. Your mother gave me too much. She thinks that I'm still young and strong, and still eat *khẻo* like an elephant. Well let's not disappoint her."

"I would like to, *Bố,* but I have to go to a birthday party."

"Oh really? But we can eat really quick, and then you can go, son."

"*Bố*, I'm late already."

"Oh all right. Well then you should go, before it is too late."

"Thank you, *Bố*."

Andy saw his father pick up a chunk of *xôi* and put it in his mouth. He chewed slowly before swallowing. Andy admired his father's honesty. He showed everything through his face. There was no holding back, like he said. Every word rushed out his mouth without a stutter. Every emotion deepened in his wrinkles and glowed in his eyes. Even the craving for *xôi* showed. Andy would have to do that later. He'd have to let everything out so Jennifer would understand how much he loved her.

Andy suddenly felt exuberant. His toes wiggled inside his socks and shoes. He really wanted to dance now. He could hear the music starting to beat inside his body. And if Andy could, he would take off all his clothes and run into the street naked, hopping like a rabbit, shaking his bare butt, and yelling, "Let's dance to my *free* love!"

Andy crossed his legs and then he spinned himself so that his face now faced the entrance of Duyen's. It was such a quick spin that it seemed like Andy didn't move, but the world had turned around for Andy. He looked at the door. The distance between him and the door shortened in his mind. Andy took a big step forward with his right leg. He tried to do the same with his left leg, but suddenly his left foot felt heavy, like a large bag of rice, and he was unable to lift it. In fact, his whole body stiffened. Andy's nose flared up in disgust.

A young couple had just entered the restaurant through the door in Andy's view. They were holding hands, making a bridge between them, a weak bridge because, in seconds, it would have to break. The girl had a beautiful face, so beautiful it was painful for Andy to look at. Her face was as bright and lively as the flowers at home in the living room. And as she smiled, a thin flower stretched between her light red lips into the dimples on her cheeks. Those were real deep dimples that were sucking the energy out of Andy. She had short black hair, so short that it revealed her tall forehead and small pretty ears. Andy glanced down to the girl's outfit. She wore a brown cotton dress that outlined her entire body. The long sleeve ran along her slender arm past her wrist and ended before touching the boy's hand.

Andy checked out the boy that was holding the girl's hand. He was all right, tall and clean and trim, but nothing too special.

The owner, Mr. Son, greeted the young couple and guided them to a table in the center of the restaurant. He gave them two menus, and only then was their bridge broken. Each of them opened the menu and looked at it, but they kept the menu low so they could glance at each other. And when their eyes met, they'd smile.

Andy sank down into his chair. He felt sick to his stomach. He turned around and faced his father, who was continuing to eat *xôi*.

"What's the matter, son?" asked his father. "I thought you were going to the birthday party."

Andy looked at his father's mouth and saw its movement, but heard nothing.

"Son, are you all right? Did you forget something?"

Andy could hear the young couple talking.

"Son?"

"No, *Bố*," answered Andy.

"No?"

"I didn't forget anything."

"Then why aren't you going?"

"It's too late."

"It's too late? Are you sure?"

Andy nodded. He looked at the plate of *xôi*. He wanted to bury his face in it.

"Hi, Andy." A voice came from behind.

Andy slowly turned his head back and looked up. He recognized the beautiful face, and refused to meet her eyes.

"I thought it was you," she said, and then she smiled innocently. But Andy refused to look at her lips.

"Hi, Jennifer," muttered Andy.

"How come you didn't go to the birthday party?" asked Jennifer.

"I . . . I was busy . . ." And Andy looked at his father,

who was looking at him. "This is my father. He works here. *Bố,* this is my school friend, Jennifer."

"Chào Bác." Jennifer greeted Andy's father, and he nodded back. "Well, you didn't miss much, Andy. The party was dead. Nobody danced. It was the music."

"Hmm . . ." said Andy.

"Everybody was late. I got there at eight but no one was there yet. You know. People didn't come until nine, ten. By that time, I got bored. You know?"

"Yeah . . ."

"I was looking for you, hoping maybe you could give me a ride home. You know?"

Stop. Stop. *I don't want to hear this,* thought Andy.

"But you weren't there. I thought you'd probably come later, so I stuck around a little longer than I wanted to. And then I met Tim over there. He goes to Andrew Hill. And Tim was bored like me. You know? And he said that he'd take me home. So we left. But we were hungry, so we decided to come here and eat. And then I saw you and . . ."

"Why are you telling me all this?" interrupted Andy.

"Huh?"

"I said why . . ." sighed Andy. "Nothing."

Jennifer looked down at Andy's eyes, and Andy looked down at her ankles.

"Well, I just thought, you know," said Jennifer.

But Andy didn't know anything anymore.

"Hey, Andy. Do you want to eat with us? I'll introduce you to Tim. He's really nice."

Still looking at her socks, Andy said, "No. I'm eating *xôi* with my father."

"*Xôi?* Well, I'll see you in school then, okay?"

"Yeah." And Andy watched her socks move away from his view until there was nothing white left but only the grayness of the floor.

"Here," said Andy's father as he pushed the plate of *xôi* toward his son.

Andy reached over and grabbed a chunk of *xôi* between his fingers, a large chunk. The rice and beans stuck to his fingernails. He placed the chunk in his mouth and pulled it away from his fingers with his teeth. His cheeks swelled up. For a moment, Andy felt a large rock in his mouth. He thought about swallowing it down and letting whatever happened happen. But he took a chance and started chewing. There was a dry bitter taste. But nothing could be as bitter as he was, so he chewed some more. The rice and beans crushed under his teeth. The bitterness faded as the *xôi* became softer in his mouth, but it was still tasteless. Andy could have swallowed now, but what the hell. Everything was already too late, so why not waste more time and chew some more. And as he chewed, he could hear the young couple talk and giggle. And their words and laughter and the sounds of his own chewing all collided and mixed into a big sticky mess. Andy realized that the words were bitter and the laughter was really tasteless, and once he began to understand this, he tasted the sweetness of *xôi* creeping out from the sides of his mouth. Andy enjoyed

swallowing the sticky mess down. Andy swallowed everything down—sweetness and bitterness and nothingness
and what he thought was love and his preparation for it,
and time.

"The forehead of that girl is very high," said Andy's father. "She must be very intelligent."

Andy nodded. Jennifer was smart enough to play with
his love. He continued eating *xôi*. With each new chunk, he
enjoyed it more and more. He even ate more than his father. He picked the plate clean with his fingers, until there
wasn't even a single grain of rice left.

"*Bố,* what did you think about when you were in reeducation camp?" asked Andy.

Andy's father stared at his son. He was surprised that his
son had actually asked him about the past.

"Oh, many things, son. Too many things. But there was
a point when I ran out of things to think about, and that
was the most frightening thing about reeducation camp. So
then every morning when I woke up, I'd immediately in-
vent something to think about for that day. I had to keep
my mind busy, otherwise, I'd go crazy."

"Couldn't you just read your own fortune to see which
day they would let you out? You said you were put in there
because you had told people what days were good to take the
boat journey. Couldn't you just do the same for yourself?"

Andy's father was momentarily quiet. He rubbed his fingers on the empty plate. Then he smiled. And then the smile
turned into a laugh. He slapped his thighs as he chuckled.

"*Bố?*"

"Son, you have discovered the weakness of all fortune tellers." And Andy's father laughed louder, louder than Andy had ever heard him laugh.

The night didn't turn out like Andy had predicted it. But he couldn't do anything about it. He drove his father home after the restaurant closed. His father praised him for keeping his car clean, a good sign for a big person. When they were home, they placed the forty *bánh trưng* in the new trash can in the backyard. Andy added the water and his father started the fire. And as they poked the wood to keep the fire going, Andy asked his father to retell the story that he told to Mrs. Thanh in the restaurant. This time his father had the whole night to tell the story. He recalled every event, his interesting inmates, the bad meals, his morning thoughts, and every invention of his imagination. And because there was time to tell the story, the story wasn't about fortunes, but about a fortune teller.

Excerpt
from *Bone*

The summer Leon found out about Tommie Hom was the
worst time. Leon came back from a forty-one-day voyage,
the first real work he'd had in over six months, with his pay
in his pocket and three stuffed koala bears in his duffel bag.
He looked good: tanned and muscled and proud to have
money for Mah. But three days later, at Portsmouth Square,
he heard about Mah and Tommie. Wives had told their
husbands, who told their park-bench buddies, who told the
Newspaper Man, who kept on telling till it was old news. So
when Jimmy Lowe went up to Leon and said, "*Wey,* Leon,
you're wearing a green hat," he thought Leon knew.

When Leon didn't show for dinner—an elaborate vegetarian feast that took Mah days to plan—Ona looked under
their bed for his duffel bag. It was gone. We assumed he'd
gotten onto a voyage, but we didn't find a good-bye note.
Leon always left some kind of note. Once he drew a ship
with a stick figure on deck, steering, and all the time he

was away, I imagined him as the captain in a peaked hat, not a shirtless laundryman with a towel around his neck. I liked it when he left notes. I liked how he signed his name. I liked how *Leon* almost looked like the twin of *Leong*. His signature reminded me of those nearly symmetrical Chinese characters: door or forest or north.

Most of the time, he left notes in Chinese for Mah. But this time he left nothing, not even his itinerary.

First thing in the morning, I called the Seaman's Union to ask which ship Leon went out on. Frank Jow barked into my ear, "What do you mean? He's right here, waiting for his number to be called."

That summer, I'd gotten a special permit through Galileo High's summer employment program and they found me a job in the catalog department of the Main Library, so I couldn't go down to the union hall to stop Leon from shipping out. Ona wanted to go. She was only ten, but she knew how to get there; she'd been there with Leon dozens of times.

Ona had no luck. Leon said he was staying at the San Fran until his number came up. When we told Mah, she didn't even take her coat off. The four of us walked down to the San Fran and took the elevator up to the ninth floor. When Leon saw Mah, he spit at her and slammed his hotel door shut. Ona cried and the door swung open again and Leon came out into the hallway and cursed Mah out. Mah started crying but Leon wouldn't stop. Doors opened and old men peered out. Nina hid behind Mah. Ona held Mah's

hand and said, "Don't cry." I stood there looking at my
shoes. The hallway was dark. It smelled awful. That's what
I kept thinking. It felt like forever, us standing there listening to Leon's whole awful story: how he spent his life waiting around at the union halls, how he worked for us and
brought home every dollar, how we were ungrateful, and
how Mah betrayed him. He said he didn't need us. He said
he didn't want Mah.

Ona was determined to show Leon how grateful she
was. She wanted to show him how much she needed him. I
think Ona probably worked the hardest at getting Leon to
come home. Every morning, she went to the San Fran and
walked with him to the union hall on Townsend Street. At
first he was embarrassed about having a child following him
into the hall, but the men liked Ona. She ran errands for
them so that they could hold on to their numbers. The job-
bers sent Ona to the corner store for sandwiches and cigarettes or the racing form, and they always told her to buy
herself a Coke, some candy. Ona said it was better than
staying home. She learned to play poker, blackjack, and
American chess. "A television hung like a fan from the ceiling," she told us. When all the jobs were filled, usually before lunch, Leon and Ona ate sandwiches on a bus-stop
bench while waiting for the number 21 bus to take them to
the employment agencies south of Market Street. Sometimes they made a detour and hunted through the Good-
will Store on Seventeenth Street, or spent the afternoon
watching old-style movies at the Grandview Theatre. Ona

loved the love stories about the butterfly lovers, fox spirits, snake goddesses, and the four great beauties. Ona told me that when they came out of the theater the afternoon sun hurt her eyes, made her dizzy.

But most of the time Leon ranted. He cursed his lousy luck: Never a good job, never a good wife. Ona listened. She was patient. Ona had stamina—his stamina—and she'd let him run his steam, and when he was done, she'd work on getting him to come home. It took about a month, but finally he agreed to a meeting. He admitted to Ona that he didn't really like living at the hotel or hanging around the union hall and the Square; he said Croney was a terrible cook. That was why he'd married Mah in the first place.

I don't remember whose idea it was to set the chairs side by side in the kitchen. I do remember the two bare wooden chairs looking like props that I've seen at the Chinese opera.

Mah and Leon sat solemnly, shoulder to shoulder, like a king and queen, and because they weren't facing each other, their furious words fell into their own laps.

Mah pleaded. She cried into her sleeve. She admitted her wrong.

Leon wouldn't look at her; he kept his hands on his knees, his eyes looked straight ahead, down the long corridor, and I imagined, maybe even out the door.

Mah said, "Everything is in the past." It was over between her and Tommie.

Stoic Leon, sad Leon. He didn't say anything. We could see him working his jaw.

Mah said she wanted to be a family again.

I watched Leon. I saw him nod.

But he didn't move back to Salmon Alley right away. For a week, Mah made him dinner and we took it to him in the same white pot we used for taking meals to Grandpa Leong. Mah began to invite Leon home for special vegetarian dinners. Leon started dropping by to fix things: the fan over the stove, a leaking faucet, a jammed window.

When he signed onto a cargo ship set for Australia, Mah looked for a new job. She thought Leon might move back if she quit Tommie's shop. She couldn't get Tommie completely out of her life because he was our landlord, and Mah couldn't imagine moving away from Salmon Alley. Leon set sail. Mah put the word out that she was looking for another factory. While Leon was still at sea, she heard about an opening at the Ching's, a much larger shop on the Mason-Taylor corner, where the cable cars made their wide turn and changed tracks. Mah loved the lively sound of the brass bells ringing. Mah started as a straight-seam seamstress, but by the time Leon returned she had been promoted to the overlock machine.

Leon did move back. A yellow cab brought him straight from the pier. I remember watching Leon lift his duffel bag out of the trunk. He looked good, tanned and smiling and relaxed. He brought us each a beaded coin purse and an alligator handbag for Mah. Friends came by and Leon gave them cubes of what he said was the world's sweetest butter. It was like a big party.

Leon and Mah never talked about Tommie Hom. We all went on trying to be a family, like Mah wanted. But things were never the same. Even their quiet was different. Leon was pensive, sad; Mah's quiet was about being afraid. Any day, I expected to come home and find an itinerary on the table, his duffel bag gone.

I have to give Leon credit, though. During that time, he tried to find steady work on land. One by one, his shipping buddies settled into steady jobs on land. Jimmy Lowe got a janitorial job at the Fairmont Hotel. Croney went to work for relatives who owned the Universal. Cousin went back to cleaning chickens at the chicken store.

Meanwhile, I helped Leon fill out his unemployment forms. *Are you physically able and willing to ship offshore now?*

Check yes, Leon said. But I could tell Leon didn't really like shipping anymore; maybe he wanted to stay home to keep a close eye on Mah, maybe it was true what he said, that he wanted to stay home to see us grow.

Will you "throw in" for every job your shipping card permits you to take?

Yes.

During the next couple of years, Leon shipped just enough to keep his card valid. Between voyages, he worked odd jobs in the hopes of finding something good enough to let his card go. He was the fry cook at Wa-jin's, the barbecue chief at Golden Dragon, a janitor in the financial district, a busboy, the night porter at The Oasis. He took a welding class and then worked the graveyard shift with Bethlehem Steel in Alameda.

All the while, Leon kept his eye open for new opportunities. He and Jimmy Lowe put in a bid for a takeout place in Vallejo. They even had a name for it: The Phoenix Walk-Away. I don't know why it didn't work out. Who knows how many more? All I know is that after Mah let Leon talk her into trying to make a go of the grocery store—while still holding on to her job at the shop—she never wanted to go into business with him again.

L. L. Grocery was on Pacific Avenue, near Powell, across from the Mobil station. Leon opened the store in the mornings while Mah sewed at the factory; Mah watched the store from four to nine, while Leon worked his graveyard shift at the steelyard. We practically lived at the grocery. I remember after school and weekends there: dusting the shelves and stocking canned goods and taking trips to the wholesaler on Stockton for paper supplies. We helped count loaves of Kilpatrick's bread as they were delivered. We rotated the milk in the refrigerator; I remember Borden's milk with the cow named Elsie. We kept the aisles stacked with salted fish and preserved turnips and dried red dates. Nina liked the baseball cards and cotton candy and Cracker Jack. Ona liked to watch the bubble-gum man count out his pennies in the back room, and she believed him when he said he'd make gum balls out of her if she broke another one of his glass fixtures.

We helped watch the store for the hour and a half between English School's letting out and Chinese School's beginning; it was enough time for Mah to do the dinner shopping. After Chinese School, we sat at the counter by the register doing our homework while Mah cooked dinner in the back room.

It wouldn't have been so bad if the store had made a profit. But business was bad. Food went stale on the shelves. Salesmen cheated Leon, smooth-talked Mah. Kids stole candy and cigarettes. I sneaked baseball cards to the boys I liked. Our only steady customers were old-timers who came by and sat on a stool by the door and read the newspaper for free. Every week, half of Leon's Bethlehem check went into the store. When I was finishing junior high, Leon sold the L. L. Grocery at a loss.

That winter, Bethlehem Steel relocated and Leon got laid off. One wild scheme followed another. Cousin told him about a bankrupt noodle factory in Sacramento. They decided to buy the machinery and dismantle it and haul it down to San Francisco to sell, but when they tried to put it back together, crucial parts had mysteriously disappeared and they ended up selling it all for scrap.

He had better luck with the coffee. When prices soared, Jimmy Lowe told Leon that he had a friend who had a friend who was looking to sell several hundred sacks of beans. Leon bought them all and went into business supplying the Chinatown pastry shops with discount coffee. He stored the sacks under the stairway and the aroma filled the apartment for a year. Once in a while, I still catch a whiff of it as I walk up the steps.

Too much dreaming, Mah said of Leon's big-money talk. But she'd lived with him long enough to understand his need to wander, to be lost in new places, new things. She shook her head, exasperated, but I don't think she ever gave up hope. She told us for a man with so many failures, Leon had a heart full of hope. Each new scheme, each voyage was his way of showing us his heart.

But Mah grew weary of Leon's schemes. She tried out her idea on me first. What if they went into business together, she and Leon? Full time. Outside Chinatown. What if they really put all their effort into something? She wanted Leon to quit shipping. She said she was ready to quit the sewing shops. I was glad to hear it. I'd watched the years of working in the sweatshops change her body. Her neck softened. Her shoulders grew heavy. Work was her whole life, and every forward stitch marked time passing. She wanted to get out before her whole life passed under the stamping needle.

When I was younger, I hated to hear Mah's confidential tone. Her words fell on me like a heavy weight. I took her questions seriously, as though it were really my choice. When I was five years old, she asked me who I preferred, Tommie Hom or Leon Leong. First, I thought to say Tommie, because something about him reminded me of the way Mah talked about my father, but I said Leon, because he brought me presents and because I knew he went out to sea. I didn't want anybody to come between me and Mah. Tommie owned most of Salmon Alley. He was always coming and going with his gangster buddies.

But over the years of listening, I learned that Mah was just lonely. All she wanted was someone to talk to. I learned to listen until I knew what she wanted, and then to tell her what she needed to hear. Maybe that's what I always did. Maybe I knew she wanted Leon more than Tommie.

Quit, I told her. Get out of the shops.

Mah also talked to Rosa Ong, who sewed beside her at Tommie's. We'd known the Ongs since they first came from Peru. They lived in an old Victorian apartment building on the corner of Jones and Pacific, which was only a couple blocks from Salmon Alley, but as far as we were concerned, that was outside Chinatown. When Rosa walked into the shop, she could barely thread the Singer, but Tommie hired her anyway and assigned Mah the job of teaching her to sew. The usual gossip started going around: Tommie had hired another pretty, know-nothing seamstress. The other ladies didn't trust Rosa because she was half Spanish, but Mah liked her pretty eyes and lilting accent, and she taught Rosa all her secret tricks to fool Tommie: what he looked for when he inspected their work (zippers), what he never looked at (darts, the hem). And when she called us to come to the factory to iron interfacing or turn sashes, she told us to do Rosa's, too.

Mah and Rosa were like sisters. They joked that they sewed more than they slept, and sewing side by side, they

were more intimate with each other than with their husbands. They had subtle rivalries. Mah envied Rosa her sunny
apartment outside Chinatown, her creamy complexion, her
long lashes, her musical laugh, but most of all, Mah envied
her her sons, Aurelio and Osvaldo. Rosa wished she could
sew as fast as Mah. She wished she could look at the sample
pattern and know all the secret seams that filled out a dress.
She envied Mah her slender brow, her small feet. She wished
Tommie liked her as much as he seemed to like Mah. (Rosa,
being a newcomer, was outside the circle of gossip and she
didn't know the whole story about Mah and Tommie.) But
mostly Rosa wished she had a daughter.

She visited us often on Salmon Alley. She and Mah
stayed up late copying dress patterns, talking about Miss
Tsai, making festival food. Rosa taught us how to crochet
and made each of us a lace shawl; we called her Auntie.

Even though they lived only three blocks away, Rosa's
husband, Luciano, always picked her up in his big black
Monte Carlo, a ship on narrow Salmon Alley. The gossip
was that he bought it with cash. The ladies all had something to say. Impossible to park. Where'd he get the
money? Does he think he's such a big shot in a black car?

Luciano Ong blew into Chinatown like a thunderstorm.
We loved looking at him in his embroidered shirts, his Sun
Yat-sen mustache. Nina liked his Ricky Ricardo hair style.
Big-boned, broad-backed, and loud-voiced, he was the
tallest man in Portsmouth Square. A crowd always gath-
ered around him to hear about his next big idea. He always

had a plan to make big money, but he always seemed to need one more grand. He was always one man short.

Luciano was Leon's kind of guy. Leon called Luciano *Dai Gor,* Big Brother. He tried to impress him with all the Spanish words he'd learned on the ships: *muchacha, maricón, calle, merengue.* He boasted about having been to South America himself, Rio de Janeiro and Santiago and Cape Horn, even to the Chinatown in Lima. Hadn't he given his last daughter a Spanish name, in honor of Columbus's fleet? (Nina was horrified.) Leon wanted to be Luciano's last man; he wanted to have the honor of giving him the grand that would make his big-money dreams come true.

Leon talked about Luc all the time. Every story he heard Luc tell at the Square he repeated for us at dinner. Luc tipped Paul Lim twenty dollars for parking his car. Luc bought snakeskin shoes at Florsheim. Luc had a gold Rolex. Soon Luc was going to buy a new Cadillac.

One night Mah accused Leon of being jealous of Luc, but Leon insisted that he wasn't. He didn't want the things Luc had, he wanted Luc's secret to success, his good fortune. That's when Mah talked to Leon about wanting to leave the sewing shop. She told him that she had been talking with Rosa about her own plans of finding a business outside Chinatown. She gave Leon the go-ahead to talk to Luc about a partnership.

The next day, he approached Luc with a proposition: fifty-fifty. Ong and Leong. Luciano liked the sound of that. Their names fit together like a pair of chopsticks that they could eat with for the rest of their lives. For weeks, they met at the Universal to read the classified ads in *The Chinese Times, The Chronicle,* and *The Examiner.* Luciano drove Leon around the city in his fancy car to look at shoe-repair shops and restaurants and a bowling alley at West Lake shopping mall. They sat in the projection booth of the Great World Movie Palace trying to bargain the price of the palace down. They negotiated with the Fong Brothers as the big machines churned out tubs of ice cream; they learned to work a photo-developing machine somewhere in the Marina.

I never saw Leon happier. Every morning he got up early and put on his double-breasted blue suit and his luck-red tie. He polished his shoes until they shone almost as brightly as Luc's. Before the sewing ladies arrived for work, Leon was at the front of the alley, waiting for Luciano.

The day they decided on the laundry, Leon came home with a whole duck and a pound of roast pork, Mah's favorites, and a strawberry cake, our favorite. In the morning, Mah withdrew their savings from the bank.

The Ong & Leong laundry was on McAllister Street, on the seedy edge of the Tenderloin. To get there, we took the number 30 Stockton bus downtown and then transferred to the 38 Geary and got off on Polk and walked two blocks past massage parlors and all-male strip joints and the Mitchell Brothers' famous theater. The storefront had two small rooms: in front there was a long wooden counter worn smooth from use and an ancient cash register, a relic from the days when the place was a retail laundry, in back, a storage room and a kitchenette where Mah made lunch. A narrow staircase led to a basement that was as wide and as deep as the belly of a ship. The first time I went down there, I stood at the bottom of the stairs and watched Leon navigate through the gloom. One by one, he found the over-hanging bulbs and pulled their strings and sent the lights swinging over each dusty machine.

Leon taught us how to twist the sheets like rope, so they wouldn't knot up while washing, and how to lift them out of the machine without straining our backs. We used both arms to carry them to the extractor, a wild spinning con-traption that whined like Dr. Joe's drill. We learned to work the press, a two-girl job. Ona and I held opposite corners of the damp sheet and slipped the edges under the hot rollers. After the edges caught, we ran around to the other end where the sheet slid out, stiff and hot and dry. We folded them by the hotel-loads, corner touching cor-ner, until each package was as tight and perfect as a new deck of cards.

It was hot down there. The humid air was chalky with starch and soap and bleach. The steam and chlorine odor clung to us. Once I smelled it on myself and was surprised with the clear memory of Leon coming home.

That summer, we were all on call for helping out at the laundry, which was almost all the time. I was taking educa-tion classes at San Francisco State University and working full time as a receptionist in the campus Career Center. Ona took classes at City College and worked the five-to-ten evening shift at Chinatown Bazaar. Nina'd just graduated from Galileo High and hadn't decided what she wanted to do yet, so she clocked in the most hours at the laundry and hated every minute of it. She said the only good thing about lifting the wet sheets was that her arms looked good in a tank top.

For Ona, Osvaldo was the best thing about Ong & Leong's. I remember watching him once. He carried two fifty-pound sacks of laundry out to the van and he tossed them through the open door as if they were goose-down pillows. He had Luc's broad back and Rosa's golden skin. Her Spanish blood gave him the dark lashes and strong jaw of a pretty-boy actor. Ona said Osvaldo looked even better than Fu Sheng, her favorite *gung fu* hero.

Soon she could time his deliveries. Somehow she could sense his presence upstairs. It was as though she could hear his footsteps above her, over the rumble of the washers. Then she wanted a Coke, or had to make a phone call or go to the bathroom or tell Mah something urgent. She'd stay up there for a half hour at a time—sometimes longer— talking to Osvaldo. When Nina complained that Ona wasn't doing her share, Mah surprised us by saying, "Let her have her fun." Leon let Ona go on deliveries with Osvaldo when it was slow. He called her Osvaldo's assistant. When there was a rush order and they needed Ona to work that extra forty minutes it would have taken her to commute to her job, Leon asked Osvaldo to drive Ona to Chinatown Bazaar.

No one was surprised to see them together upstairs, sitting on top of a pile of laundry bags and holding hands. Mah made only one rule. She asked Ona to please not sit on his lap in the front of the store where anyone walking by could see. Ona did it anyway, but as a gesture to respect Mah's wishes, she pushed the big rubber plant in front of the window. Leon started calling Osvaldo "son," and Mah and Rosa giggled about being sisters.

Ong & Leong inherited the previous owners' hotel clientele, but Luc took it on himself to drum up more business. He called himself the marketing manager, the outside man. He called Leon the plant manager. Leon was the inside man in charge of the whole washing operation. Mah told Leon to go with Luc to the hotels once in a while to learn the business end of things, which was her way of telling him to keep an eye on Luc, but Leon said he was too busy. Luc was the talker and Leon was the worker. Leon claimed he liked it that way.

When there was a lull, Ona and Nina and I always ran upstairs to sit in the light by the big front window. But not Leon. He liked it down there with his machines. The sound of all the washers going, the extractors spinning, the dryers hissing, calmed him. Mah said it was as if he was in the engine room of his own ship. She took his dinner down to him, a big soup bowl piled high with rice and vegetables, and he'd walk around, his bowl balanced in his palm, listening to his machines. He knew every machine by its sound. He said that each motor had a different voice, and he could tell when one was getting tired, ready to break down.

All summer, one by one, they all did break down. Leon always got them working again somehow, but we worried, especially Mah. Would the dryers be hot enough? Would the extractors spin? Would we make the deadline?

Then Ong & Leong's went bust. We had no warning. Luc kept the books; we never saw the summonses or the eviction notices or the unpaid utility bills. We found out one rainy Saturday morning in late November when we arrived and found the place padlocked shut. None of our keys worked. I held an umbrella over Leon as he called Luc from the corner phone booth, but there was no answer. Leon slammed the phone down so hard he cracked the earpiece.

We knew not to ask anything right then. I knew the money was gone. Leon and Luc had only shaken hands on the deal. There was no contract, no legal partnership. I blamed myself. I should have done more; I should have made them go to a lawyer to set the business up. But I hadn't. Mah and Leon seemed so high on the idea, I didn't want to bring in doubt. It was their business, and if they wanted to do things the Chinatown way, if they wanted to depend on old-world trust, I didn't think it was my place to interfere.

Leon went looking for Luc, which was also the old-world way. He didn't show for dinner. Midnight. Still no Leon. We didn't say what we were all afraid of. Ona wanted to call Osvaldo, but Mah wouldn't let her. We sat together in the living room. We waited until two o'clock and then Mah told us to go to bed.

I lay in bed, trying not to fall asleep.

Mah's hoarse voice scared me awake. "Why did it come to this? How could it come to this?"

We knew to stay in our rooms. We listened and the footsteps told us enough: Mah's slippers slapping from bathroom to kitchen to bedroom and Leon's heavy boots dragging down the hall. Their bedroom door shut and then we could only catch the high and low pitches of sound changing; screams and low groans and then a steady silence.

Leon stayed in his room for two days. Mah brought him his meals. She wanted to call a doctor, but Leon said no. Mah went and found Rosa and flew into a fury. Rosa played innocent: She had no idea; she had no power over her husband, no knowledge of the details. So Mah fumed at us.

I told her, "Don't think about it. It's over now."

Trust, the old-world way. We hadn't been paid for the five months of work we'd put in, and all our savings were gone. I asked for a month's advance pay from my job. Ona was paid in cash every Friday. Mah asked Mr. Ching for her old job, but he'd already hired another seamstress, so Mah went back to Tommie's.

We didn't talk about Leon's bruised and swollen face or his limp. We left him alone and soon his sullenness spread through the apartment. Maybe our quiet was a way to express our own fear and sense of disbelief, of defeat. I'd had my own dreams for the laundry, that a successful business would bring Mah and Leon back together in a deeper way. Around then, a letter came from my father, wanting to make contact, a long-lost, rekindling letter, but there was too much happening for me to feel anything for someone as far away as Australia. I was getting close to Mason and I wanted my own life. I didn't want to worry about Mah or Leon or anybody else.

Ona worried me in a way I couldn't let go of. I always felt that she had the most to lose. She was too sensitive, too close to Leon. When she was little, she'd be weepy for days after Leon left on a voyage, and she'd wait for him, shadowy and pensive, counting off the days till he came home. Every time he lost a job, she went into a depression with him. When he got high on some scheme, she was drunk on it, too. Mah said she was like Leon that way: Ona had no skin.

I think Nina had the best attitude. Leon's problems were his and Mah's were hers, and she hated Chinatown and she was getting out.

Leon started coming and going at strange hours. He spent his days at the park, or with his buddies at the Universal or the Jackson Cafe. Evenings, he wandered around Waverly Place, visiting the chess clubs. He'd come home way after midnight, and then he always cooked up a snack. It confused my dreams to smell rice steaming with salted fish.

When Mah tried to talk to him, he turned on her, blaming her for everything. "Your fault. Women's talk, sewing-lady gossip."

I should have seen it coming: Leon turned on Ona, too. He told her to break up with Osvaldo. "I forbid you to see that mongrel boy. Crooked father, crooked son."

Nina told Ona, "Just say whatever Leon needs to hear. Then you can do whatever you want." I agreed but Ona refused to lie. She told Leon she loved Osvaldo.

Leon threatened to disown her. "You will no longer be my daughter. I will no longer be your father."

What did he think, this was like a divorce? Just because he said something it would be true? But in a strange way, after those words came out of his mouth, it was all over. Forbidding Ona was like daring her.

Leon was relentless. His frustration went deeper than losing the laundry. He blamed himself for the humiliation. And every time he saw Osvaldo, he remembered his whole past, every job he got fired from, every business that failed. He hung up on Osvaldo, refused to let him into the house. He yelled at Ona every night all through dinner. The harder Leon pressed, the tighter Ona and Osvaldo became.

Once Leon blocked her at the door. He said, "I'm warning you! If you go, don't bother coming back!"

That night, Leon did lock her out. So Ona spent the night at Osvaldo's. Maybe that's when she started to keep secrets. Maybe she figured the less any of us knew, the better.

Then the Ongs moved out to the Richmond district and Ona spent even more time there. We hardly saw her. I heard that it was Luc who put in the call that got Ona her job at The Traders.

I worried about her. Not only because she was Leon's target, but also because she didn't have an out.

The thing that stuck in my mind was what Ona told me about how she felt outside Chinatown. She never felt comfortable, even with the Chinese crowd that Osvaldo hung around with; she never felt like she fit in.

My out was Mason. Nina had a part-time job at Kentucky Fried Chicken on Bay, near Tower Records.

Mah told Leon that Ona would outgrow Osvaldo. I tried talking to him; Nina did too. We even got Cousin to tell him to let up on Ona, but Leon turned on everyone. I started hoping that Leon would ship out: I thought a voyage might clear his head.

At work one day, I took a job call for a dishwasher at the University of San Francisco Medical Center. I took a chance and sent Leon. I figured, How can he fuck up a dishwashing interview?

But in my desperation to get Leon out of the house I didn't even consider the obvious—they'd called a student employment office, they'd expect a student.

Leon came home in a rage. "They asked if I had experience!" he fumed. "Who doesn't have experience washing dishes?"

But they offered Leon the job and it seemed to give him some balance. It calmed him, but I knew that would pass.

❀

The night everything finally blew up, I realized it had been inevitable, but all week I'd been too tired to see the warning signs. Ona had been with Osvaldo for three nights. Leon had some problem with his supervisor. I was beat from work and beat from staying out late with Mason. I came home glad that dinner was ready; all I wanted to do was eat and then go to bed. Leon came in just as we finished eating. Mah had put some dinner aside for him. She went to heat it up.

Then there was a knock and Ona was going down the hall and it was Osvaldo standing there, Osvaldo bending forward, Osvaldo kissing Ona.

It happened fast: Leon getting up and going down the hall after Ona. Ona rushing out the door and Leon following her. Then I ran after them and Mah's scared voice was behind me, asking, "What's happening? What's happening?"

I stopped at the top of the stairs. I saw Leon yank the car door open and reach in, grabbing at Ona. Doors opened up and down the alley. Lights came on.

But Ona kept fighting him. She pushed and flung her arms, she hit him. Leon was yelling something in Chinese, but I couldn't make out what. Mah started yelling too; she tried to rush down, but I blocked her and told her, "No!" I didn't want her hysteria to feed his.

Ona's screams filled the entire alley.

Osvaldo yelled, "Leave her alone!"

But Leon wouldn't acknowledge Osvaldo. He kept yelling at Ona, "You better listen to me, I'm warning you, if you want to be my daughter, you better listen."

"Leave her alone," Osvaldo shouted again. He got into the car; the engine turned over.

From the top of the stairs, I saw the neighbors back away from their windows, turn off their lights, shut their doors. The alley darkened, became very still. I could barely make out Leon's shadow. Then Osvaldo's headlights flashed on and flooded the alley for a second before sweeping away onto Pacific Avenue. It was only one swift moment of light, but it lasted long enough for me to see Leon looking after Ona as if he was watching everything he'd ever hoped for disappear.

PETER
BACHO
• • • • • • •

A Matter
of Faith

When the phone rang, I knew I should've let it be. Bad news travels at two A.M. Still, I picked up the receiver, driven by habit, not caution or sense.

"Buddy," the voice said.

"Hi, Mom," I said, trying to sound cherry. "What's up?"

"Buddy," she said sadly. "It doesn't look good . . ."

My heart dropped; I could barely make a sound. "What?" I finally said. It was the best I could do.

"Your Uncle Kikoy. He went to intensive last night, you know, for his heart. He wants to see you," she said. "Just in case."

I loved my mom, but I learned from my dad and his cronies (like Kikoy, one of my bachelor uncles on my mother's side), those stylish, confident, generous men who taught and protected me, kept me safe. Wherever. Chinatown cardrooms, flophouses. Wherever. But for those happy, secure times there's a price to pay. I will mourn more than the passing of two parents. Kikoy, I know, is just the first of many.

"They're all going, Buddy . . ." She started to cry. "Every week we attend funerals. Seems that's all we do. All the old-timers, our friends."

I sighed. "I'll be up, Mom," I said as I reviewed my mental ledger, not much at eighteen. Some cash in, more cash out. What was left I was saving—or trying to save—for college.

Flying was out of the question; on such short notice, the cost would be crazy. Alternative two: Greenie, my dad's old beater. I wondered if it could make the trip, maybe its last, from Frisco to Seattle. Fortunately my dad wasn't around to say no. He was spending Christmas vacation in Reno with his new wife, Victoria, a young girl from the Philippines much closer to my age than to his.

Greenie might not return. But for this, one way was enough. The trip would be tough, no doubt, but I had no choice. I'd explain it to Dad later. Uncle Kikoy was family, the bottom line.

"Buddy," she said. "When you coming?"

"Soon as I can," I said as I recalled other motor trips north. I'd done it before, at least a few times, but never alone, and never in December. Silently I computed costs: gas, oil, tuneup, food . . . Scratch food, just drive straight through. "Two days," I assured her. "Three days max."

"Buddy," she sighed, "he might not last that long."

"Tell 'im to wait," I said. "Kikoy will wait, just tell 'im it's a matter of faith, his boy's comin' home."

It's a matter of faith, I thought as I ran through the automatic doors and into the lobby of the V.A. Hospital. Kikoy had been a sniper in the Pacific, his job to pick off remnants of the Japanese Army in the jungles of Borneo, Samar, and Leyte. He enjoyed his work. "When I aim, they see their ancestors," he'd say proudly. He'd laugh—more a high-pitched giggle—and roll up his right sleeve to show a scar in mid-biceps. "Of course, they try to make me see mine. But, you see, I'm not dead, 'cause I got faith." He'd point to his heart. "In here, Buddy, in here."

In that sense Kikoy was different from most of the other old-timers, an irreligious lot. I never saw him in a church, but he believed in God, and summoned Him periodically. "You got problems, Buddy," he'd say solemnly, "you ask for help. It'll come. The Japanese, they shoot at me, but they miss, 'cause I believe. It's a matter of faith." On those occasions (and they were several), I'd nod, feigning agreement. Even as a child I wasn't religious, as a teenager even less so. I saw no need for God—He was illogical, worse, inconvenient, especially after I'd started dating—a diet of Catholic schools notwithstanding.

Still, I survived those days and around my neck hung a memento from an earlier time, a small Saint Christopher's medal Kikoy gave me when I turned eight. He said he was wearing it the day he was shot. Legend said St. Chris, the patron of travelers, had once carried the baby Jesus across waters that swept away all before them—dead and alive.

Kikoy swore the medal had saved him, brought him home from the war. But now he was old (almost sixty) and getting older. Not even saints could stop the movement of time. I, however, had a long way to go. And on that road—he promised—Chris could be helpful.

Out of respect I wore the medal, but in ten years had never invoked the power of my protector. A narrow, unbending logic was enough; all else was superstition. Still, during that time I'd also never removed it, and had managed to survive bouts of violence and recklessness ("acting out," the school psychologist said) that started just after my parents broke up, and I'd moved to Frisco with Dad. It was a choice powered more by economics than affection; my mom, with the twins, Willy and Toni, six years younger than me, couldn't afford us all. As the eldest, I had no choice; four years ago they needed her more.

The burden of duty, of being the eldest, produced something else. Bad attitude marked the first three years, starting with my first hour in the new city (I'd threatened a cabbie who tried to shortchange me after a ride from the airport).

About a year ago, I finally changed after a ten-day stay in juvy during which I nursed two swollen eyes and pondered a rap sheet that was starting to grow. As I lay in my bunk, I finally realized that I could never piece together my parents' broken love. Dad, I figured, was moving on, and Victoria, his child bride, was clear (if embarrassing) proof of this. I knew I had to do likewise; at eighteen, the period of youthful criminal grace vanishes down a bottomless funnel of adult crimes and institutions. I knew several who were too smart, or so they said. They laughed their way through juvy but, as adults, weren't laughing now. I watched as they slid down the funnel, and swore I wouldn't join them. That meant college, even a j.c., of which my sporadic attempts to save money were part.

The medal dangled from my neck on the morning I raced from the parking lot to the hospital where my uncle lay, maybe minutes from death. I was late. It took three days alone to gather the money, buy the parts, do the repairs. Even then, nothing was assured.

"Nurse it," Junior had said. At thirty, he was a reformed car thief and, like many of his trade, a superb underground mechanic, maybe the best in Frisco. He was the older brother of Herbie, my best friend and former partner in juvenile crime. Junior ran an unlicensed cash-only garage out of their parents' house and was so good, his customers included lawyers, judges, even cops. His folks, two old retired Filipino immigrants, pleased that their wayward eldest had managed to stay out of jail, gladly provided him space, choosing to ignore the more obscure legal dangers of unreported income. I guess they figured that given a choice, free but illegal enterprise was better than careening car chases.

When we weren't courting trouble, Herbie and I would hang around the shop and watch Junior squeeze miles out of rusting engine blocks. Two years ago Greenie's odometer froze at a quarter of a million miles; I needed a few more.

He frowned as I counted the bills just drawn from my now depleted college account. "Two hundred," I finally said, and thrust the cash toward him.

Junior just shook his head and made no move to accept payment. "Did the best I could, bro," he said. "But I can't guarantee . . ."

"Got a chance?"

Junior shrugged. "A chance," he said. "Donner Party had a chance."

"Wrong mountains," I said.

"Principle's the same," he replied. Although he laughed, he'd made his point. Even with a new car, a midwinter trip through the mountains was never easy.

"A chance's all I need," I said, and again tried to hand him the money.

Junior shook his head. "Nah, it's all uphill from Redding on," he said, referring to the long winding route from northern California to central Oregon. "You get stuck there, brother, you'll need all the coin you got. That happens, man, stay away from hungry-lookin', toothless hillbillies. They'll eat you, Benny, it's cultural." He paused. "Pay me when you get back."

"Junior, man," I stuttered as I tried to thank him.

"Forget it," he said. "From one Flip to another. Means I understand. Got uncles like Kikoy. Different names, same situation. Go on. If you're like me, you owe 'im."

The trip became a twenty-hour ordeal. Along the way I'd stop to call. Status checks. The last being Grants Pass at midnight, ten hours earlier. "He's okay," my mother said, "resting, but hurry."

I did the best I could, particularly with the oil leak that sprang as I crossed into Washington. With one eye on the oil light, the other on the road, I ignored the grind of metal on metal and a headache that screeched almost as loud. Somehow I shut it all out and pressed on, never stopping, didn't dare to, especially in the homestretch—from Tacoma to Seattle—when Greenie sputtered forward on will and occasional bursts of downhill momentum.

One more time, Junior's magic had worked. I'm not sure how he did it—maybe duct tape, Superglue, and two novenas. Maybe Saint Chris. What mattered was that faithful Greenie—now a collection of loosely joined parts—was in the lot, and I stood by the front desk in the lobby.

"Kikoy's room," I blurted to the receptionist, a bored-looking black woman chewing vigorously on a large wad of gum. Cow with cud, I thought. She was staring at the last down column of a newspaper crossword of middle-school simplicity. I glanced at the desk: a five-letter synonym for "fake."

"Pardon me?"

"I'm sorry," I said, trying to gather myself. "I mean . . . Rodriguez, Mr. Rodriguez." I just realized I never knew Uncle Kikoy's real first name.

"Which one?" she asked blandly, without looking up. She was tapping her pencil and thumbing through a small pocket dictionary. "We have many patients with that last name, at least four as of yesterday."

Damn, I thought. I didn't know his first name. To me he'd always been Kikoy, a nickname. For Filipinos, nicknames meant closeness, a key granting access to the intimate. I didn't know his real name, didn't have to. I blanked and looked nervously at the clock, trying not to look dumber than the woman in front of me.

"Never mind," I finally said. "What's the floor for intensive?"

"Third floor." She yawned and pointed to the elevator down the hall.

As I hurried toward the twin elevator doors, I turned toward the desk. "Try 'phony,' " I yelled at the woman. She looked up, unsure. "You know," I added, "like the folks that work here."

The elevator opened to the third floor and a familiar voice. "Wait," the voice commanded before I could exit. A thick right hand firmly grabbed the edge of one door, keeping it open for my mother to enter, followed by Uncle Rey, her older brother. Downcast, at first they didn't notice me, surely a bad sign.

"Mom," I whispered.

She looked up. "Buddy," she cried as she hugged me. My uncle, retired army, was always more reserved; he patted me on the shoulder. "He's gone," she said sadly. "You missed him. He asked and he asked, and I told him to hang on, that you're coming, but he couldn't . . ."

"Mom," I said as I gently tried to loosen her grip, "I should at least see the body, do somethin' . . ."

"Can't," she said. "Body's gone, moved it an hour ago.

There's nothing more to do." She paused and managed a faint smile. "Let's go home. Willy and Toni, they're waiting . . ."

"Damn," I whispered. Going on hope and its helpers— caffeine and adrenaline—I'd finally run out. Busted car, broken spirit. Legs shaking, I leaned against the wall, too tired to stand, too sad to move. My system was shutting down. "Damn." It was all I could say.

"Just come on home, son," my mom said as she grabbed my arm. "You need to rest. Don't worry about Uncle Kikoy, he knows you tried. I told him you were coming, and he'd smile. As the end got closer, I'd tell him, beg him to hang on. And he'd still smile, though I'm not sure he even heard the words."

My mom paused and pulled me closer. "Just before he died," she whispered, "he said something to me. He knows I'm religious, just like him. Rey's not." I glanced at my uncle, who stood away from us, back straight, hands folded, eyes focused on the elevator doors. At sixty plus, he was a proud, still physical man who fought the frailties of age—the crooked fingers, the curved backs of his friends. Mom claimed he willed his bones to stay straight, and I believe her. His hear- ing, though, was another matter. It was almost gone. He had a hearing aid, but pride kept it out of his ear and in a drawer.

"Go ahead, Mom," I said in a normal tone.

"Anyway, he doesn't know," she said, still whispering. She nodded at my uncle. "Rey was out in the hall. Kikoy said, 'Tell Benny, don' worry,' he says. 'I'll see 'im. I got faith, but he gotta have it, too.' "

I stared at her blankly.

She shrugged. "Exact words," she said.

As the elevator doors opened, my uncle suddenly turned to me. "Just come home and rest," he said. "Think about tomorrow, tomorrow. Nothing more to do here."

"Nothin' more to do," I managed to mumble. "Least not here."

The twins were at home as promised, eager, happy, smiling. Normal. They shrieked and grabbed, peppering me with questions. How was I doing? How was Dad? Why didn't he come? Somehow I responded without incriminating either our star-struck, foolish father or myself, using answers culled from police interrogations: shrugs, nods, one-word replies. Eventually the twins released me, distracted by the pungent scent of pork adobo wafting from the kitchen. Me, I was too tired to eat, even adobo, and used this reprieve to walk the short distance to my room, remove my clothes, pull back the covers, and collapse on the bed, so drained I felt I may never awaken. Cool, I thought, closed my eyes, and dropped off.

In the dark my heart raced. I could hear it, louder and faster, revving to the level I knew it couldn't keep. Then what? Wake up, I thought, and turn it down.

My eyes opened to adjust to a dim light from two small candles on the desk by the wall of my old bedroom. I glanced at my watch: almost midnight, twelve hours of sleep, a lot. I stared at the tiny flames that flanked a small picture of Jesus, His heart wounded and choked by a crown of thorns. No doubt my mom's handiwork. She believed in prayer, of which lit candles and religious pictures were a form. Each room in the house had a similar shrine, although mine had been removed from the onset of puberty at thirteen—when I found sex (or at least sexual thoughts) and lost the last shards of a diminished faith—to the day I left home. Fire hazard, I'd successfully argued. Now, after an absence of years, my mother was back to her tricks, praying for me even while she slept.

I smiled at the thought, God or no, and smiled also at the other lessons that this kind, believing woman tried vainly to impart. I couldn't remember them all, there were so many, tangled like a collection of old fishing line. I'd sort them out in the morning, too tired to ponder religion, the meaning of my racing heart, or any other matter.

As I started to slide back under the covers, first one candle extinguished. I blinked. Odd. No flicker, no sign the flame would soon go out. Then the second. Same way. Eerie, much worse than odd. I bolted back up, my mind racing to find an answer, a logical one. Fatigue, imagination, bad eyesight? Maybe a breeze? A quick scan of the walls searched for open windows; slight cracks would do. Then I remembered. My religious mother was also energy conscious—this house was hermetically sealed—a double paned PG&E temple.

I slumped in the bed, out of answers, except those I didn't want. Eyes open, too scared to sleep, I could only breathe and stare. A small lamp on the bed stand tempted me; electricity could break this dark, superstitious grip. Light could bring answers, buy time enough to rationalize and reduce, maybe even forget. I reached for the switch, then stopped. What if light explained nothing? I withdrew my hand.

I loved him and wanted to see him, but at what cost? Should I invoke St. Chris to bring him, my uncle, now a phantom, not flesh and bone? Then what? Attend church, or relearn rules and rituals long dismissed as inconvenient bunk?

Grabbing the medal, I ripped it from my neck. I held it up to a dim thread of street-lamp light, filtered weakly through double glass panes. I closed my eyes and felt the contours of St. Chris, hoping for answers.

The medal was a gift from family, an act of kindness, one of many not yet repaid. And here was a chance. Uncle Kikoy was family, the bottom line; I owed him. For the first time that night I relaxed, then laughed. All this fuss, and there was really no choice. Carefully, I laid the medal on the bed stand and got ready to pay a debt.

I closed my eyes and could feel my palms dampen. I hesitated, gripped by no small fear. Again, my heart started to pound, revving like a modified Detroit V-8 legend on Saturday night. Breathing deeply, I gathered myself and plunged ahead.

For family, the bottom line.

"Just bring 'im, St. Chris," I said, hearing my words over my own internal din. Then silence, broken by a faint sound, probably imagined—a trace of a giggle, a high-pitched one.

I gulped. "Bring 'im," I whispered.

About the
Contributors

PETER BACHO is a teacher, journalist, and attorney who lives in San Francisco. He has published stories in many magazines and is the author of the novel *Cebu,* as well as a collection of short stories underscoring his Filipino heritage.

LAN SAMANTHA CHANG is a first-generation Chinese American who was born and raised in Appleton, Wisconsin. She is currently a Fellow in the Creative Writing Program at Stanford University. Her fiction has been anthologized in *The Best American Short Stories 1994.*

MARY F. CHEN is a writer of fiction and nonfiction whose work has appeared in *The Literary Review,* among other publications.

CYNTHIA KADOHATA is a Japanese-American novelist whose work has been widely anthologized in the United

States. She is the author of the novels *The Floating World* and *In the Heart of the Valley of Love*.

MARIE G. LEE is the author of *Finding My Voice*, for which she won the Friends of American Writers award; her other novels include *Saying Goodbye* and *If It Hadn't Been For You, Yoon Juu*.

KATHERINE MIN is a short-story writer whose work has appeared in numerous publications, including *The Beloit Fiction Journal, River Styx,* and *Ploughshares*.

FAE MYENNE NG was born in San Francisco and now lives in New York City. Her short stories have appeared in *Harper's* as well as other magazines. She is the author of *Bone,* a novel.

NGUYEN DUC MINH is a Vietnamese writer who lives in California. His fiction has appeared in various magazines, including *A*.

RYAN OBA teaches English at Santa Monica College and cofounded the Asian American Playhouse at Cornell University. His poems and short stories have been published in numerous small magazines.

LOIS-ANN YAMANAKA's first novel, *Wild Meat and the Bully Burgers,* will be published in 1995.